T H R E E

S Q U I R T

Three
Squirt
Dog

D O G

THREE SQUIRT DOG

Rick Ridgway

St. Martin's Press
New York

THREE SQUIRT DOG.

Production Editor: David Stanford Burr
Design by Judith A. Stagnitto

Library of Congress Cataloging-in-Publication Data
Ridgway, Rick.
    Three squirt dog / Rick Ridgway.
            p. cm.
        ISBN 0-312-11079-0
        1. Man-woman relationships—United States—
Fiction. 2. Young men—United States—Fiction. I.
Title.
    PS3568.I35924T48 1994
    813´.54—dc20   94-2037
                                                 CIP

First Edition: June 1994

10   9   8   7   6   5   4   3   2   1

FOR PHYLLIS,

WITH ALL MY LOVE

Part
One

MAD-DOGGIN'

I celebrated my twenty-first birthday not with my family, nor with my best friend and lover Jane, but with my oldest, least trustworthy, most triumphantly irresponsible buddies, Zak and Tony.

Tony appointed himself the designated driver and agreed to stick with Budweiser in moderation (two six-packs maximum). Zak and I rode in the backseat, our feet sinking into crushed cans, discarded clothing, concert programs, and other debris from recent and ancient debauches. We had six bottles of Mad Dog on the floor next to Tony's beer cooler.

It was June the 8th. The air smelled as sweet as perfumed titties. Girls in shorts were taking their evening strolls, and Tony cruised slowly on the leaf-shaded streets so that we could ogle them at our ease.

There was steady suspense. Some girls looked great fifty yards away, but like squawk-birds up close. Others had braces or potato noses or spindly legs or quicksand thighs. Some of the snootier strollers provoked Tony into beeping his horn, a customized blast that approximated the riff from Led Zeppelin's "Rock and

Roll." It shocked these Heights princesses—being honked at by a lustmobile full of baboons, one of whom (Zak) hung his gob out the window and mimed cunnilingus.

We hit the nine o'clock showing of *The Road Warrior* at a $1.50 flea-pit on Mayfield Road. Two reasons for the discount price: the ticket taker was a dead ringer for the commandant in *Seven Beauties,* and the artificial popcorn butter smelled rancid enough to rot your stomach lining. Naturally, Zak bought a jumbo tub. He had a bottle of Mad Dog in his jacket pocket and needed something crunchy for ballast.

The movie was a kinetic spree. In his wine-boosted euphoria Zak relished the Gyro Captain—his jagged teeth, his goofy courtliness, his pterodactyl agility. I preferred the Warrior Woman, who looked like Jane with added height and subtracted softness and irony. We all enjoyed the terrible mohawked Wez, though he was no more fearsome than a high school jock on a steroid-and-Old-Milwaukee bender.

The outback dust blew and the jabbering stray kid whirled his boomerang and the crazed vehicular mayhem escalated and a seductive six-bit nihilism prevailed. It was a damn good movie, and an antidote to the placid delicacies of another Australian movie I'd seen recently—*Picnic at Hanging Rock.* Which was all flute music, honeyed sunlight, virgin schoolgirls in white undies, and mysticism. Aussies were definitely more likable when they had a wild hair up their ass.

The audience raved like a lynch mob when Wez latched onto the speeding bus. Gumdrops were hurled. Some enthusiastic black guys up front shouted advice to Mad Max—

"Shoot that feather-boy…"

"Cut the wheel…"

"Ram that mo-fo…"

We exited at eleven and began to cruise around. Tony had a Budweiser between his knees and Zak hung his head out the window like a carsick mutt, lapping air. I had a puddle of Mad Dog souring in my stomach, and it was in a territorial dispute with a clot of chop suey that I'd had for supper. There was not enough space in my gut for happy coexistence, and I was anticipating the projectile puking that would signal the official outbreak of war.

We headed south into the countryside, far from the depressingly uniform facades of Fast-Food Alley, and parked with the lights out under an apple tree. Frogs made a thick porridge of noise—there must be wetlands nearby.

"Hit me with a beer," Tony said. I passed him a can, as Zak knocked him on the shoulder. "Keep that puke-hound under control back there, Bud."

"I'm gonna do my Mount Vesuvius thing pretty soon," Zak threatened. "Right on you—Bud Carew."

"It better be just popcorn and wine," I said.

"He'd never skip dinner," Tony said.

"What else did you eat, Zak?"

"Cheese and salsa and taco chips—and a big fuckin' bowla clam chowder."

"Weeping Jesus. It's gonna smell like the freakin' puke apocalypse in here. Help him aim, Bud."

"I may blow, too, Tony. Watch out for the firestorm effect."

"Come on. You got a cast-iron stomach. Hell, you put up with Omar on a daily basis."

He meant my bastardly younger brother, Omar, who was fifteen.

"Happy birthday, Bud," Zak said. He handed me a second bottle of Mad Dog. "Howzit feel t'be an adult?"

"I haven't felt like one yet."

Tony squeezed his can flat and pitched it at our feet. "Hit me. I'm gonna need an anaesthetic just to tolerate you fuckers."

Zak nudged Tony's arm, gurgling ominously. I passed Tony a beer. Then Zak's chin dropped onto the windowsill and he barfed a landslide down the back door.

"There goes my paint job."

I dipped a wad of Kleenex into Tony's cooler and used it to swab Zak's chin. Tony clicked a flashlight on and jacklighted Zak. Pink chunks of potato and clam dribbled down his shirt. I swabbed his bib and flipped the disgusto swab out into the orchard.

"Zak, suppose you have to attend an upscale function," I said. "Future Gas-Station Attendants of America meet Princess Di, say... How will you get by without disgracing yourself?"

"I know my Emily fuckin'-Post. Uhhhhiiikkk." He hawkered out the window. "Always apologize when you puke on a lady."

"Yeah, but suppose you whip out your snotrag t'give it to her, and it's all encrusted with dry snotshots? It'll mortify Di."

"I'm no barbarian. I'd offer her my shirttail. Fuck, I'd take off my whole shirt and give it to her."

"Yeah, the armpits are like moist towelettes," Tony said.

As Zak chuckled, a thin pink gruel started to ooze from his nostrils. "You fuckin' guys."

"Turn the light off," I said. "Before I have to watch his ears leak."

Tony finished a six-pack and decided to abstain for the rest of the night, leaving the other six on ice. Zak tilted his third bottle of Mad Dog and chugged. I dipped two dirty socks in ice water and tied them together and wrapped them around Zak's head to cool his brain. We all de-carred and took a steaming piss in the grass.

We drove home at two A.M. Tony's headlights lit the rosebushes along our driveway. I felt queasy getting out, but I was confident that I could make it indoors and puke in solo dignity.

"See ya, Bud," Tony said. "The movie was almost good enough to cancel out this puke-weasel."

"S'long, birthday boy," Zak sputtered. He dangled his head out the window and retched another gallon on the driveway.

"You wretched fucker," Tony said.

"Thanks a lot, Zak," I said and reeled into the house. I heard Tony's jalopy backfiring up the street and some outback war whoops.

I made it to the back bathroom, which was really a closet-sized hole behind my bedroom, and upchucked for about five minutes. I rinsed my burning mouth and throat out and soaked my head in cold water. I crawled into bed wet-faced and slept in the fumes of my own stupidity.

Twenty-one, a college graduate with a buttwipe B.A. in English, no solid employment prospects. I was pretty happy.

OMAR

Toward wake-up time I dreamt the last few shots of a dream-movie: in the blue-green Mediterranean, panicky bulldogs were dog-paddling and woofing. A slob on a yacht banged a barrel against the hull. He wore a gory apron and a long-billed cap. He pitched a metal lid at a bobbing bulldog, and just before the lid hit the water or the dog, I woke up with a swarming headache and an acid-hot stomach.

It was eleven-thirty and my cowboy-and-Indian-patterned curtains were aglow with sunlight and shaking in the June breeze. I swallowed three aspirins and some tap water and flooded my face and head again.

I heard the front door open. Thirty seconds later the needle landed on the Ramones' *Rocket to Russia* album. My headache expanded a notch. I went up the hall naked to the master bathroom and climbed in the shower. I tried hot (painful), cold (shocking) and lukewarm. Nothing helped. My head thrummed and my stomach queased.

I dried off and put some blue-jean cutoffs on and went into the living room and cut the stereo volume from seven to five.

"Next time ask, Muzak-face," Omar said. He was frying Vienna sausages in a skillet full of melted oleo. His pal Kevin, the guitar player in Omar's band, was squirting ketchup into raggedly split pita bread.

"Want some lunch?" Omar asked.

"What's it look like? Turn the coffeepot on why doncha."

"Dewey says to hose down the puke—and you're s'posed to take me and Kevin to Burger King for supper. He left a ten spot on the counter. He's got a record convention to go to. Not gonna be home till after nine."

"Great."

I sat on the couch cradling my head. Omar and Kevin, instinctive sadists, carried their sandwiches into the living room and made me watch them eat. Omar swigged chocolate milk from the carton and passed it to Kevin.

Kevin had marfed-up sausage and wet ketchupy bread going in and out of his mouth like a magic trick. I pressed my palms against my eyelids and rubbed until I saw a dim Jackson Pollock painting shuddering on the insides of my eyelids.

I walked dizzily to the kitchen and standing up had two cups of coffee. Now I had a caffeine pulse jackhammering inside me to complement my headache. I fixed an icebag and sprawled on the couch with the ice pressed to my forehead. Freeze the bastard out.

Omar showed some pity. He set the volume back to four and put on Warren Zevon's *Excitable Boy* album. Zevon might've been the only singer-songwriter Omar didn't loathe. The scruffiest groups were his great love. Dewey had weaned the obnoxious little shit on the Thirteenth Floor Elevators and the Flamin' Groovies.

Omar knew the lyrics to "Roland the Headless Thompson Gunner" and did a passable singalong when the cut came up. My headache was dissolving. Thank you, Lord. I will suck the toes of lepers if You do something about my dyspepsia.

The phone rang and Omar answered it belligerently. "It's Jane the Pain," he said.

I took the call in my bedroom. "Sweet baby," I pleaded. "Forgive me or I'll kill myself."

"Let me consider that." I heard her chuckle and I relaxed. The paradisaical smells of grass and blossoms wafted in, and my stomach settled to a mere dull discomfort. I might find religion yet—some rogue pro-fucking, pro-rock 'n' roll, pro-drunkenness sect.

"Here's the good news," Jane continued. "My mom'll be gone all afternoon and Freddie's went tubing. The house is ours."

"Wonderful. Give me a half hour to shave and brush my teeth and all that shit, then I'll be over. I have to be back at six to take Omar to Hamburger Hell for his daily beef ration."

"Okay. You'll like your presents."

"Jane, I'm sorry about last night. They're my oldest friends. It would've devastated them to get drunk without me."

"I know, I know. You're the glue that binds them to any trace of civilization. What is Zak gonna do if his parents kick him out?"

"You tell me."

"Fix yourself up and get over here quick. I've been touching myself all morning..." Jane chuckled her low catwoman chuckle that made my blood go tropical.

"Hey, start without me. I'll catch up."

"Bye."

7 shaved and brushed and gargled and de-odorized my pits and put on a clean shirt and sandals.

"I'll see you rats' asses at six," I said to Omar and Kevin. They were eating jellybeans and pulling records out of the orange crate—the Dictators and the Sensational Alex Harvey Band. I was leaving just in time.

A squadron of flies and gnats buzzbombed Zak's puke puddle. I turned on the hose and blasted the wad into the grass until it became a few pink shreds of clover-killing noxiousness. I hit it with more spray, shooting it onto an anthill near the weedy border of our side lawn. This was inhumane to the ants or possibly nourishing. I left it for the worker ants to sort out.

As I dragged the hose back toward the house, I saw Sideways Sam, our neighbor's black-and-white mongrel, scurrying along the ditch. "Sorry I trashed your lunch, Sam," I said. "You'll have to duke it out with the ants." Sam was the proverbial shit-eating, car-chasing dog. Having careened off scores of passing cars, he survived with his crooked-legged, sideways lope. Lucky he lived on a dead-end street.

Sam had black ditch mud on his snout. He might've been hunting for sala-manders or frogs. I know that he'd eat anything. Bonnie, his owner, once dropped a Bermuda onion on the floor: Sam snatched it and consumed it in ten seconds flat, chewing it as Bonnie clobbered him on the puss and tried to pry open his jaws with their wet pink-and-black folds of slobbery skin.

Bonnie came out on her porch now. She was a 280-pounder in a violet muumuu and clogs—a shrewd, friendly widow with three lummox sons.

"Afternoon," I called.

Bonnie squinted in the harsh   *10*   sunlight, her sizable forearm lifted to block the glare. "Hi Bud. Get over here, Sam…Did you hear O.T. drive up a minute ago or am I going crazy?"

"I may be going crazy myself. Omar's had the Ramones on and outside noise doesn't penetrate. I haven't seen O.T. all week."

"That shitbird. He was supposed to shop. Do you guys have any jalapeños in your fridge?"

"Might have. Dewey likes 'em."

"I'm gonna come over and check. I'm in a nachos mood. Have lunch with me."

"I can't, Bonnie. Gotta go see Jane."

"Shucks." She waddled across the lawn, carrying a paperback book. It was *The Last Gentleman*, which she'd borrowed the previous week. Our friendship had started years ago when Bonnie lent me two lemons and a copy of *The Man Who Loved Children,* and we'd been passing books and foodstuffs back and forth ever since.

"Tremendous book." She handed me the dog-eared paperback.

"It's one of my favorites. Go on in and Omar'll help you find the jalapeños." I got in my car and tossed *The Last Gentleman* on the backseat and slid the car out around the rocks. As I got up to speed on the gravel, Sam came tear-assing at me and pinged off the passenger door in back.

In the rearview mirror I could see him sitting in the tall ditch grass, panting and grinning and dipping his head to lick his pecker.

BUD LOVES
JANE

*J*ane's house was packed in tightly on a shady suburban street, not affording maximum privacy or discretion. Some neighborhood biddy might notice my car and pass on the info to Jane's parents, who didn't like me much. I parked my car at a 7-Eleven and walked the last three blocks.

I rang the bell and waited on the hot, sunny porch, my blood heating up to match. My dick was snorkeling up through my shorts. I waited. I rang again.

Jane finally appeared. She was wearing a pink silk nightgown. I ducked inside and swept her up and bent the three inches it took to make our mouths level and kissed her. My heart was a jackrabbit scooting in circles.

"I see you've been thinking about me." Jane lightly brushed my erection with her hand. Static electricity from her silk nightie crackled, making the hairs on my wrists tingle as I felt the shape of her waist. "D'ju crash your car?"

"Abandoned it. Let's go upstairs before I have an accident and go hacky on your mammy's throw rug."

Jane's room was away from the sun. Cool blue colors. A framed print of Takanobu's "Portrait of Taira Shigemori." On the bed table a paperback of *Dad* and a glass of grape pop.

I cast off my shirt and sandals and flattened out on Jane's comfortable queen-size bed and watched her with joy. She slipped off her nightgown and stood in her light-mocha June tan, her small breasts and round butt white. She twirled once, flashing me, and got on the bed, kneeling beside me and chuckling.

She put her hands inside my shorts and grasped my dick like a baton. I tore my cutoffs and shorts off. Jane straddled me backwards, her ass looming above me, and licked and teased my belly. Then she turned with feline grace and slid up my chest and kissed me on the lips.

I tasted grape and sweet saliva. Against my chest I felt her hard nipples. I had my hands in her hair, which was a thick cloud of chestnut and dark blonde. Her eyebrows were a darker shade of brown, like varnish, and her eyes were luminous brown, soulful. How her parents made such a merry, carnal beauty was one of life's happy mysteries.

Jane wiggled higher in bed, giving me her pink nipples to suck, knowing it would drive me nuts. I stroked two fingers over her thigh and between her legs and felt that she was wet. Holding her by the hips, I eased her downward and fitted her atop me and was inside her. Thrilling moist heat. She clutched me with her pussy. As Jane seesawed on me, she inclined her mouth so that I could rock upward and kiss her. She nipped my lip. Yips and lower growls shook loose in her throat. Leaning back from her kiss, I cupped her breasts and felt the pliant responsiveness of her skin. So beautiful. I had to shut my eyes as they began to tear up.

I kept stroking, more rapidly now to match Jane's fierce passion. Silently I thanked the designer of all bodies for every nerve ending, every sculpted piece of flesh. My fingertips tingling, I caressed Jane's ass, which had its unique hard-soft texture.

I couldn't hold it. My sperm was bucking and leaping and percolating. I came in a long surge, my eyes wincing shut with impossible pleasure overload, my nerve endings from scalp to toes shouting hallelujahs of praise.

We lay in an embrace, murmuring, Jane's hair tickling my chest. I didn't have enough breath to kiss her for about two minutes. Her lips trembled as she murmured and her eyes were shut. I kissed her shoulders and neck and breasts. Her nipples were still hard and I could feel the stirred electricity when I held her hand. Jane's body was humming. A flesh dynamo. She pressed the inside of her thigh against my leg and I could feel how wet she was, how ▮ stirred.

"Wanton," I said.

"You bet." Jane's eyes batted open. She smiled and kissed my nipples, which were hard as buttons, too. How we loved to feast on each other. I stroked her thick mass of hair. I swallowed and felt my heart grow calmer. Amazing that all that thunder and excitement didn't obliterate us. We lay still, delicately touching, and dozed together for a minute or two in our sweet fuck-daze.

Jane made a small gurgle of private laughter. She cupped my kneecap. "I'm glad it was you that showed up and not the UPS guy," she said.

I laughed into the damp pillow. "If he only knew. He'd crawl across a desert of broken glass and give a year's wages to trade places with me."

Jane rolled out of bed and put Joni Mitchell's *The Hissing of Summer Lawns* in her tape player. It wasn't one of my favorites, but it didn't matter. I was so happy that I would've gladly listened to Lydia Lunch or Wild Man Fisher.

I welcomed Jane back into bed, the merest brush of her skin stoking the heat inside me. She played idly with my erection and pinched me near the waistline. "The beginning of a fat handle. You need an exercise program, mister."

"This *is* my exercise program. The hell with the discus and the javelin. I need to make love to your sweet body on a daily basis, then we can hit the Olympic trials in August."

"What an ego."

"Ego schmego. I just like things that feel good and look good and smell good and taste good…It's sensual craving. It's in my genes…Cake, for instance. My mom used to make this devil's food cake with cherries and whipped cream. God, that fuckin' thing tasted delicious. When I was about eight years old she made one of these deals and put in on the counter. I smelled it and I snuck in and ran my fingers into it and gouged out some whipped cream and cherries. My mom caught me and she just laughed. 'You're just like me, Bud,' she said. 'Sensually greedy.' And she took a big swipe with her fingers, too. Then she refrosted the fucker...And that's the way I am—one of the greedy, devouring Carews. I won't even mention my dad. If he'd walked into the kitchen he might've eaten the whole goddamn cake on the spot."

"Hmmm. So I'm just cake in human form, am I?" Jane smiled. She almost always smiled when she teased me.

"Yes. Organic, sensual, spiritual cake. And I'll never get tired of tasting you." I licked Jane's tummy, tobogganed around her navel, slurped upward until I encountered a nipple, and stopped to suck it. "A rosette on the cake."

Jane pinched my ass. "Let me up so I can give you your present." I watched her, beautifully nude and languid, skim aside a scarf on her dresser and pluck a small rectangular box wrapped in candycane paper. She set it on my thigh. I peeled it open and found a tape of Alex Chilton's *Live in London*, an obscure import that Dewey had been trying to find for me without success.

"This is great, Jane. How'd you find it?"

"Babette the Girl Wonder got it for me in London."

"How'd she manage to get a passport? She's got a rap sheet." Babette dressed like Elvira, Mistress of the Dark, and was rumored to be a kleptomaniac.

Jane squeezed my balls. "Watch it with the character assassinations, mister. She lifted one lousy perfume when she was about twelve."

"I hate to risk an injury to my cubes, but wasn't she busted for disseminating Anaïs Nin literature a ways back?"

Jane scoffed. "That's bullshit and you know it. Anaïs Nin is a much better writer than some of your Monkey Island literary heroes."

"Like who?"

"Like the spermbrain from Brooklyn, Henry Miller."

I covered my sac with both hands and said, "Anaïs could probably knit better baby booties than Henry. But outwrite him? Never."

Jane nipped me lightly on the shoulder. She maneuvered until she was on top of me and pushed her palms into my biceps. The touch of her warm skin made my dick lift and graze her haunch.

"If you quit maligning Babette and Anaïs, I'll give you your other present."

"Okay."

Jane slid off my chest and angled her feet over the baseboard and tickled my thighs with her hanging tendrils of hair. Jesus, what an anticipatory sensation that is! Jane kissed my dick, then slipped her lips over it. Her hands feathered my torso, skimmed over my chest. I shut my eyes and submitted as she licked and sucked me. When I was close to eruption, she let me slide from her mouth. She got on top of me and bronco-bucked me to a lollapalooza of an orgasm.

It took me awhile to reagain my senses. Name? Bud Carew. Place? Jane's room. Date? 6-9-83. Feeling? Total erotic and romantic bliss, gratitude, wipeout.

I cradled her in my arms. "Jane?"

"Hmmmm?"

"What's stronger than love?"

"I don't know. What?"

"Whatever it is, that's what I'm feeling for you. Not just now but permanently."

"One great blowjob and I'm stuck with you forever, huh?" She chuckled, squeezing against me. "Do you renounce Satan?"

"Yes."

"Do you renounce Henry Miller?"

"No." I held Jane's hands so that she couldn't attack, and when she tried to nip me I intercepted her and kissed her.

BODY

FUNCTIONS

I plodded back to my car at 5:45 and it was as hot as a cauldron. I'd misplaced my sunglasses and I had to concentrate hard on the bright highway, which glowed like an ingot. Jane's emanations were making me tender and groggy. I couldn't see her again until Friday, and my body was suffering a form of erotic bends instead of the deep well-being of fifteen minutes earlier. I would have to marry Jane or else volunteer for castration. Too much torment in the absences. And her vindictive parents were threatening to take her to Cape Cod shortly. I would have to swoop along the Atlantic beach and spirit Jane away with helicopters in pursuit. HARD-ON HANG GLIDER GRABS BATHER.

When I got home, Omar and Kevin had their instruments plugged in and the house vibrated with amplified din. A ghost of my headache returned. I realized suddenly that the last food I'd eaten was the water chestnuts, mucky gravy and fried noodles of twenty-four hours ago. The appetite-imp was clog-dancing in my stomach and cackling: burger, burger, burger...

Kevin and Omar piled into the backseat and Kevin leaned forward to dog-breath my neck as I drove. Like Omar, he was fifteen and ratty and proud of his rattiness.

"What's this shit?" Omar said, lifting and examining the Alex Chilton tape.

"It's a sacred object. Don't fuck with it."

"How much ya pay me if I don't smash the case and chew the tape loose?"

"Omar—here's a gentle suggestion. Investigate another facet of your personality for a change. You're overworking the destructive asshole side."

"Smells funky in here. Did you jack off?"

Kevin snorted, spraying my 17 neck with mouthjuice.

"Settle back, Kev—I need a dry neck t'drive. Omar—cool it." I borrowed Jane's anti-Henry smear. "You're probably smelling the fluid in your brain."

"Fat chance I'll stop. How's Jane the Drain doin'? Bet she dumps you before the summer's out."

"Slug him for me, Kev. I can't reach him." They thrashed around, pummeling each other.

"Hong Kong nerd whammy," Omar said, dusting Kevin's skull with his knuckles.

At Burger King we stood in line in the grungy foyer behind a dozen other burger-addicts. It had a glum bureaucratic ambience: tallowish fluorescent lighting, potted rubber plant, shit-brown tile floor, listless register jockeys in shit-brown uniforms.

"Gimme your orders now so I don't have to suffer the humiliation of standing in line with you two DNA mistakes."

Omar: "Listen close, bush-head—cheese Whopper fries chocolate shake cherry pie. Make that two cherry pies."

Kevin: "Plain Whopper onion rings large Pepsi cherry pie."

It cost thirteen bucks for the two trays of crap. I tried to squeeze the lemon wedge into my iced tea, and it was juiceless. Omar ate his French fries like a baby bird eating earthworms. He swiped one of Kevin's onion rings, causing a swift slap-fight. I longed wistfully for a dab of elegance. Both gluttons sucked their drinks dry vehemently, vacuuming the bottoms of the cups clean.

"See that dweeb clearing tables?" Omar said.

Kevin wiped a runnel of ketchup from his chin. "Yeah, who is that guy?"

"Remember the Schnogs? That guy played drums for 'em. They did one Friday hop and they started fightin' on stage 'cause they couldn't agree on what songs to play."

"Too much airplane glue and not enough rehearsal."

"Drummed like he learned how to on an oatmeal box."

"His kit was for shit…He was in ▮▮▮▮ another band later."

"Puppysnuff. 'Member them?"

"Vaguely."

Omar was adept at tracing the history of amateur bands in the area. He was always recognizing and trashing rival punk musicians.

"What are schnogs, anyway?" Kevin asked.

"I think they're guys with warts on their balls or somethin' like that." Omar horked up some milkshake, one nostril seeping pale brown bubbles, as Kevin wheezed along in harmony.

"You'd be better off with warts on your pud," Omar added. "Save money on French ticklers."

"When are you pud-pullers gonna get a gig?" I asked.

"Next Friday night," Omar said. "You're not invited."

"That's a relief."

"Unless you wanna be our opening act. You could sing folk songs, and everybody could heave dogshit at you."

"No, I'll let 'em save the turdballs for you guys. What are you gonna call yourselves?"

"The Butt-Stabbers."

I sucked a little iced tea and it tasted like boiled tennis shoes. Evidently Burger King scrubbed its teapot about once a decade.

"You schmos wanna play a little miniature golf, get some cultural activity in before sundown?"

"Fuck no," Omar said. He farted violently.

Kevin shook with silent mirth.

Body functions, I thought. We're nothing but body functions.

DEWEY

9:45. I was plopped on the couch reading *The Bushwhacked Piano* and was at the point where the psychotic surgeon was about to perform a hemorrhoid operation. I heard Dewey pull into the garage. He came through the breezeway and called, "Hey Bud. Get over those intestinal squitters?"

"Yeah."

"Where's Omar?"

"In his room with the headphones on. I invoked the Motorhead headphones-only rule."

"That should be a permanent house rule."

Dewey strolled into the kitchen, carrying a foot-long Mister Hero cheesesteak and a six-pack of Rolling Rock. I marked my place in *The Bushwhacked Piano,* saving Payne's comic ordeal for after midnight. I got up to stretch. Dewey plugged in the electric bun warmer, unwrapped his sandwich, and packed it into the warmer slant-wise. He got his jumbo Slurpee cup from the dish rack and poured two beers into it.

"Abstaining tonight, or d'ya feel heroic, Bud?" He gave me his possum grin.

"Might have one just to cleanse my system. If I let you drink all six beers, you'll be up all night peeing."

"Yeah. You better help me out. I'm peein' more and enjoyin' it less already. When you hit forty your hose starts to turn into a sprinkler system."

I took a beer. Dewey moseyed up the hall to his bedroom, and undressed and pulled on his Bermuda shorts and Black Sabbath T-shirt. I tossed the book onto my bed. Dewey opened Omar's door and crept to the foot of the bed and tickled Omar's feet.

We settled in the living room. Crickets had a steady rasp going in the bushes. Otherwise it was quiet.

"Find anything good at the convention?"

"Couple bargains. Mint copy of Richard Thompson's *Human Fly* album and some Tim Buckley in pretty good shape. I sold those Chocolate Watch Band albums. Got us some beer money for a couple of months."

"That's a shame. Those are good records."

"I got 'em taped from earlier copies. I think Rhino's gonna do a *Best Of* on them, too." He took a big swallow of Rolling Rock. "That suds goin' down okay?"

"Tastes fine. That puddle was Zak's, by the way."

"Jesus! I was afraid I was gonna get stuck in that sucker and have to call Triple A."

"What can I say? Zak eats like a warthog and can't hold his wine. He's a menace to the community."

"Bud, *nobody* can hold that cheap swill down."

"That's true. That wine's evil."

"I wonder if Mad Dog was around in Nietzsche's time. Old Fred might've had a thing or two t'say about the malign attraction of Mad Dog."

"Burns like fucking turpentine when it comes through your nose, but at least I managed t'hit the pot with mine."

Dewey finished his beer and went to the kitchen to pour another double. He flipped me the last can, and I caught it against the lampshade. He put his cheesesteak on a paper towel and spread the front page of the *Plain Dealer* across his lap and started chewing. No one in our family ever willingly used plates or silverware.

Dewey was my dad Roy's younger brother. He was forty-five and, like my dad, strictly a non-disciplinarian. When my dad keeled over dead four years ago, Dewey took us in cheerfully and did his best to help us over our distress. He owned a record store and was a lifetime music lover. My dad had loved classical exclusively, but Dewey's taste ran in all directions: from John Lee Hooker and Muddy Waters to Bartók and Stravinsky, from John Coltrane and Ornette Coleman to the Clash and Joy Division. I could come home in the evening and find him and Omar on the couch, eating macaroni and listening to the Sex Pistols, both singing along with macaroni chugging in their cuds to "Anarchy in the U.K."

We bullshitted until Dewey went to bed at 11:30. I had to get up at 8:30 and go to work with him tomorrow, since his ace assistant Charles was taking the day off. I retired to my room and put the Alex Chilton tape in the deck and stretched out with my headphones on. The performances had spirit, even though Alex's voice was mostly wrecked, and there were a couple songs I'd never heard before.

I put in Prince's *Dirty Mind* next. I tried to teleport myself to Jane's bedroom and failed miserably. Stuck on my bed with insomnia and an erection, I listened to a custom-made Sandy Denny tape. I loved these songs, but they tranquilized me enough so that I hit the OFF button and shut my eyes for the day. I could smell Jane on my skin—soap, perfume, hair, flesh, sexual juices. I curled up like a lonely embryo and inhaled my chest hairs. I wouldn't take another shower until I got home from work tomorrow.

RECORD BIZ

$\mathcal{D}$ewey's store was in the heart of the Boho district in Cleveland Heights. He let me drive so that he could read the box scores at leisure and drink coffee from his Slurpee cup.

"What'd the Tribe do?"

"Lost six to one to the Tigers... Dave Kingman hit two homers for the Mets. Inject a new personality into that guy and teach him to field a position, you'd have something."

"He's a gorilla."

I parked and Dewey unlocked the store and switched the lights on. We didn't open officially until ten. We had time to make more coffee and frig around.

"Recite the oath," Dewey challenged me.

"Do not buy Journey, do not buy Rush, do not buy Styx, do not buy REO Speedwagon. Go easy on the haircut bands—no one will want to own Kajagoogoo in the near future."

"Pretty good. Add BTO and Grand Funk Railroad to the list. Everybody seems to be liquidating those. And remember to look closely for scratches and grit and dried peanut butter."

"I don't understand the Rush embargo, Dew. Granted, they don't appeal to us finer types. But they were always popular with my high school peers. At least they can play their instruments. The singer *is* a nightmarish screecher..."

"This may be true. But we got too much of 'em in the bin already. Have to maintain a flow."

"It's a wonder you get anything good. Who's gonna sell their Robyn Hitchcock collection?"

"You'd be amazed, my boy," Dewey said in his W. C. Fields voice. "Some of these bozos get desperate for getaway money, they'll sell their copy of *I Often Dream of Trains* for fifty cents."

Penny rapped on the window and Dewey let her in. Near thirty, she still looked nineteen. She had on her usual Annie Hall outfit—in fact her dress code predated *Annie Hall*—and rimless specs. She was smoking a cigarillo. Penny was one of the few decent-looking women I'd ever met with whom I absolutely could not imagine myself in bed.

"Bud, you look tired."

"I am tired."

She put a Mike Oldfield record on the behind-the-counter turntable, but kept the volume low so as not to agitate Dewey and me too severely. Dewey let her and

Charles run the store for the most part. Charles had worked here for ten years and Penny for eight. It was a good situation all the way around.

"Charles is cunt-struck again, I fear," Penny said to me. She had a cup of mint tea and another cigarillo going.

Penny's vocabulary often startled me. I once heard her say, "Christ, does my twat itch," and another time, "I'm having an especially nasty cramp in my cooze. Hold down the register while I go take a pill." She wasn't catty or malicious or eager to shock, but she was disarming in her directness.

I mulled over her "cunt-struck" remark and said finally, "It's not a bad condition to be in."

"Don't get smug, Bud. You wait. We all have claws and we'll use 'em eventually."

I hooted. "Listen to these tigress threats...Jane trims her nails. She's heaven-sent and true blue."

Penny squinted through her rank cloud of smoke. "You sound like some Broadway puddin'head lyricist, Bud. There's danger afoot here. And I can't imagine you ever getting along with Jane's parents."

"I won't argue that point. Terrence I can *almost* relate to, except he babbles about golden oldies constantly. He thinks Huey 'Piano' Smith is New Wave. But Ellie—she downright hates me. She looks at me like I'm a white slaver or a morphine pusher. Whatta I have to do to convince her? Hire a skywriter to write I LOVE JANE AND I'LL NEVER HURT HER above their house? The fact that I make Jane happy is like an *affront* to old Ellie. And furthermore—" I paused to let Penny get a giggle in.

"And furthermore, how could I ever trust a woman who drinks elderberry wine spritzers or cranberry juice and hamster piss—whatever the hell that red swill is that she's always got a glass of. And not even a glass. Some skinny-ass little antique figurine miniaturized goblet. At least Terrence drinks a beer now and then. And the worst thing is, she's got those skinny chicken arms and she wears a shitload of hoop bracelets and arm accessories so that she looks like a walking Slinky toy. I bet Terrence hasn't given her a good fuck in human memory..."

Penny shot me a look of burning reproval. "You *are* smug. You think that you and Jane are the only lovers on the planet, huh? Did you invent some wild new form of sexual gymnastics?"

"Oh don't pry, Rona," I said in an effeminate voice. Penny whacked me on the arm, giggling and coughing smoke. I held up my hands in self defense. "I'm not attacking their entire sexual history. Jane's a love child, she has to be. Ellie musta got Terrence drunk and put on a pink garter belt or something back in the good old days before she mutated into a liver-spotted chicken lady." Penny kicked my shin and backed away a couple paces. "So congratulations to Terrence for firing that one primo wad. But he also shot the diseased spunk that resulted in Freddie."

"Freddie's no worse than a generically monstrous fifteen-year-old American male. He's in that swingin'-on-a-rubber-tire, jackin'-off-in-a-sweatsock phase. He'll start to assume human form shortly."

"Talk about smug. You never had a fifteen-year-old brother and you're spewing all these anthropological conclusions like Margaret Mead..."

"Snap out of it, Bud! I got groped by a *score* of fifteen-year-old yard apes. I remember fifteen very vividly. Give me some credit."

"It's ten o'clock. Let's open up. I'm a little bedazzled trying to picture this score of gropers. How many is that? Twenty?"

"Believe me, I was *groped*." Penny took the keys off the hook and opened the door. Immediately a kid who looked like he'd spent the night in a Dumpster slipped in with a stack of Jefferson Starship and Chicago albums. With a dire expression Penny examined them, rejected several of the worn ones, and paid $5 for the remainder.

I tagged them at $4 apiece and strolled out into the aisle and racked them. Chicago had a thick section in front of Chilliwack and behind Chic. The Jefferson Starship was sandwiched by Jay and the Americans and dull, grinding old

Jethro Tull. There was a lot of shitty music on record. The worst bands were like obese, ugly, smelly, ill-tempered people: no redeeming qualities.

Penny sat owlishly in her smokescreen. She gave me the finger, then smiled. "Smug-o," she called.

I took my handkerchief out and waved it in surrender, then swept it off my hand with a flourish, revealing an upthrust middle finger.

"Smug *and* a treaty-breaker," Penny said.

I lingered by the import bin, pawing through picture discs and gaudily packaged singles and EPs. I was no Anglophile, but the Brits coughed up a fair share of zanies and visionaries. At least they were unpredictable.

Customers came in and Penny rang up a bunch of sales. She even peddled a used turntable to a guy in a goatee and beret who looked like Dom DeLuise.

"Was that Dom DeLuise?" I called.

"No, I think it was Sebastian Cabot."

At noon Dewey emerged from his office in back and hit the running tote key on the register. $465. He was satisfied enough to buy us lunch. He went up the street to the deli and returned with pastrami sandwiches. We took turns scarfing lunch at the table in his office, and Penny spent an hour reading *Falconer* while Dewey and I manned the register.

It stayed busy all afternoon. People were buying tapes to play on those long summer drives. I sold lots of Van Halen. Eddie Van Halen irked me—Mister Fast Fingers. I thought of Truman Capote's sniping putdown of Jack Kerouac: not writing, but typing. Which was unfair to spontaneous Jack, but *sounded* authoritative. Eddie Van Halen was a speed typist trapped in the body of a guitar player.

One customer, a slender girl with long pale-blonde hair and glittery blue-green eyes (both spooked *and* spaced), asked me to help her. She had a list of records that her kid brother owned, and wanted to augment his collection appropriately. It was a depressing list: Boston, Yes, the inevi-

table Rush, Asia, Kiss. I steered her to

our new acquisitions: two Chicago and two Jefferson Starship, adding some Queen, Foreigner and a couple Rush he didn't have. Feeling guilty, I threw in Echo & the Bunnymen's *Crocodiles* album, just to give the miserable kid a taste of weirdness. It was a $60 sale, my best of the day.

At 6:30 Tony came in. "Is the Meat Loaf under 'Meat' or 'Loaf?' " he asked Penny.

"It's under Big Fat Sweaty Guys. With Canned Heat and Barry White."

Dewey let me knock off for the day. I drove up to the park with Tony and we sat at a picnic bench and drank Dr Pepper. We gossiped until the sun began to fade.

"Is Zak back on solid food, or is he still spewin'?"

"You won't believe it," Tony said. "He got a job at Pellardi's on the night shift. Grocery stocker."

"What a kick in the balls. I thought he was gonna take a course in mechanics. I guess it'll keep him off the streets five nights a week, anyway."

"Four. They do ten-hour shifts."

"Wow. So Zak found a vocation. Makes me feel shiftless."

"He can probably get you on too. He knows the manager pretty well."

"Piss on that idea. I like being unemployed."

"Why don't you work for Dewey full-time?"

"Ahhh...I might some day. But I can't screw Charles and Penny out of hours. I'll do Saturdays and an occasional fill-in like today. That's enough."

"Mr. Ambition.... What if Jane wants to be wined and dined in style?"

"She's not a little bitch obsessed with money. We're happy the way it is."

"Whatever you do, promise me one thing, Bud—no marriage. It's poison."

"Shit. Not with Jane, it wouldn't be. We all look at marriage by the example of our parents. We get to see the worse shit up close. It's gotta be better than that, Tony. The idea is not to repeat their stupid-ass blunders. Can't human beings learn *anything*? I'm prone to be as cynical as you are, but not about *Jane*. Christ, I'm only twenty-one. I don't wanna be a defeated old man...until I get to be one." We both chortled. "And it's not inevitable. Dewey's still got some life in him. My dad bopped till he dropped. And you know how my mom was. She was emotionally demanding. She was irrational. She was capricious. She was nuts. She *is* nuts. What can I do, disown her? I love my mom…"

"Does she write you at all?"

"She *calls*. She's a compulsive telephone talker. I'd hate to see her phone bill, because most of her friends still live in Ohio. Maybe Baba-Whatever-the-Fuck-His-Name-Is foots the bill." My mom lived on a commune outside Corvallis, Oregon. She was forty-three years old—a giddy, manic, restless, dissatisfied woman.

"Nobody has sane parents," Tony said. "My dad's losin' his rocks day by day. I hope he can make it to fifty-five and retire."

"Hang in there with him no matter how fucked up he gets…I have to get back and give Dewey a ride home. Let's catch a movie tomorrow. *Local Hero* is supposed to be good. How's the nine o'clocker sound?"

"Good. Pick me up around 8:40. I'm fuckin' outta gas until payday." Tony worked at his dad's auto-body shop.

Storm clouds obscured the sunset and it was already twilight in the trees. A girl in crimson shorts climbing a far knoll looked supernatural, her golden hair stirring in the rain wind, her arms windmilling strangely. In the western sky there was lightning as we walked back to the car. I drove Tony home to his house on Lee Road—he had walked to the store—and went back to pick up Dewey.

"Took in over a thousand. Bonuses all around." He handed Rolling Rocks to Penny and me.

Waiting for
the Weekend

Wednesday was uneventful except for the pleasure of seeing *Local Hero.* Everybody in the movie was so off center that it made the notion of being *on* center seem priggish. All day Thursday, I had fantasies about making love to Jane on Friday. They were even raunchier than playmate or movie-starlet fantasies—they were more *specific,* including details of touch and taste and scent that even the most dedicated erotomaniac couldn't conjure when fiddling with imaginary lovemates. I kept active, so as to curb my intoxication—both imagined and actual sex could make me punch-drunk, silly.

After the dew burned off at midmorning, I mowed the lawn. We had two acres, and I had to steer around the beds of perennials and roses and Dewey's vegetable garden (which the rabbits had been raiding already). I ate a sandwich at one o'clock, then went back out to weed the borders along the driveway.

Across the street was the Steingruber house. Bob Steingruber was a widower and a traveling salesman. I saw three newspapers on his stoop. When Bob was home he liked to sit on his porch, his gut tumbling over his belt, and blast down a six-pack, with Perez Prado or Martin Denny coming scratchily through the speaker he had in his window. As I weeded, I saw Sideways Sam trot down the road and detour blithely into Bob's defenseless yard. He squatted and crapped. Bob needed to booby-trap his property with some spring-loaded mechanical dogshit sensors.

I sat on a chaise lounge and chugged some of Omar's cherry Kool-Aid and finished *The Bushwhacked Piano.* I hand-washed a few shirts and hung them on the clothesline in the backyard. I hated going to the goddamn laundromat in the summer, which was why I owned at least forty pairs of socks and shorts.

Omar dropped in briefly to get his case of pics and his Big Chief tablet covered with lyrics. Each song was an ode to aggression or an outright psycho spree. "My Dog Will Eat Your Lips," "Rusty Spike in the Head," "Nosebleed Blues for Youse," "We're All Goons." His first band, when he was thirteen, was named It's Your Turn in the Barrel, Darrell—debunking guitar-flunkout Little Darrell Lahoud. I pitied the poor overmatched teachers, doctors, social workers, or prison officials who might have to deal with Omar in the future.

Late in the afternoon I boiled some spinach pasta and mixed vegetables and cooled them. Then I added cheese chunks and vinaigrette to make a cold salad for Dewey and me. Omar could fend for himself—I knew he wouldn't eat salad unless it had a pound of bacon crumbled into it. Let Kevin's folks lay down some slops for the hungry power trio. Their drummer Jack—who, like all rock drummers, looked like he survived on a diet of live white mice—was practicing with them in Kevin's garage.

I listened to R.E.M.'s *Chronic Town* for about the hundredth time, then the Cramps' *Songs the Lord Taught Us* and Elvis Costello's *Armed Forces*. I was hungry, but waited for Dewey to get home.

He came in at 8:20 and took a quick shower. We sat on the couch eating salad and rolls, drinking rum and Coke, and watching the Indians battle the White Sox. When the Tribe fell behind by five runs, we switched to music. Dewey was feeling mellow. He picked Brahms's *Horn Trio*. The cricket sounds and the frogs from the mini-lagoon behind Bob's house made it a quintet.

Omar called at 9:30 and asked Dewey if he could stay all night at Kevin's. Sure. We celebrated this turn of events with another round of rum and Coke. Dewey put on Stravinsky's *Symphony of Psalms* which, even as a heathen, I loved.

At ten we checked back with the Tribe. They had closed the score to 9–8. We watched them go ahead 11–9, then lose 12–11 in the bottom of the ninth when that big four-eyed clumse, Ron Kittle, jacked a three-run homer.

"Two outs in the last of the ninth and blotto!" Dewey said. "Rooting for the Indians is like going to a singles' bar for thirty years and not getting laid *once*."

"Might as well get inured to celibacy, Dew."

I stumbled out into the kitchen to fix us rum and Coke number five.

Dewey sighed when I handed him his drink. "Celibacy is the worst. I need t'do some work."

"What's Meg been up to? Avoiding you? Or dodging around with a gigolo?" Meg was an attractive, flaky divorcée, Kentucky born, who drove a schoolbus. I'd seen her bus many times, going like hell, Meg with a butt dangling from the corner of her mouth, brats in a tumult up and down the aisle. She wouldn't waste her breath yelling at them.

"Ah, she went home to visit after school let out. She'll be back at the end of the month."

The rum had knocked me a little loopy. "Still beat your meat at forty-five?" I grinned helplessly.

"Hell yeah! Can't let it go inactive...I swipe a *Penthouse* from Omar's stash t'get a clear inspiration. No sense whackin' off to old memories. Stretch marks and sags. Hell, there's some unbelievable women in those magazines. I like t'read the little bios, too. Personalizes it..." He winked. "Hope Omar doesn't jerk himself to death before he hits sixteen."

"You're okay, Dew."

He chuckled. "It'd break my fat old heart if you disapproved, Bud. Imagine a nephew lecturing his uncle about the dangers of masturbation." We downed our drinks and Dewey went to bed.

I took a cool shower to discourage my rum-boosted hard-on. I tried to read a Flannery O'Connor story, but was too groggy to concentrate. I shut off the light and began to think inevitably about Jane.

Jane had been a grade behind me   in school—a skinny girl who, at seventeen, fell within the dreaded category of "cute." When I was away at Ohio University as a freshman, Jane grew three inches and filled out to 115 pounds and became a heartbreaker-beauty. When I came home in December of 1980 and went with Tony to hear Tom Waits sing at a dive in the Flats, we ran into Jane and her friend Barbara, a scornful poodle-cut blonde. We asked them to sit with us and bought them drinks at $2.50 a pop.

Jane was not flirtatious or fidgety. She paid attention to the music. Waits was in fine grumbling form, wearing an Irish derby, a striped polo shirt, and an iridescent green jacket. Backed by an upright bass, acoustic guitar, and drums, he diddled the piano keys and rasped a slew of booze-soaked ballads and shaggy-dog stories. I know Tony was bored—his taste ran strictly to guitar bands—and Barbara got huffy when Waits did "Pasties and a G-string," but Jane and I were rapt.

Our dough was running low, but we had enough to buy scrambled eggs and ham at Denny's. (I recommend this fare for neutralizing mild forms of drunkenness.) Jane drank coffee calmly. Tony had to vent some of his pent-up rock 'n' roll fury: he scooped up his eggs on two halves of an English muffin and ate the rubbery mess in three bites. Jane seemed more amazed than disgusted. We lingered in the cold parking lot, trying to impress the girls with our sardonic teenage bullshit. Barbara, reluctantly I think, drove Tony home, and I went with Jane.

I made only a couple small jokes on the drive. When I got to Jane's house, it was ablaze with Christmas lights. I could smell her hair and her perfume and her skin. I almost lunged at her and kissed her. These jungle tactics had worked a couple times on the Athens campus. There was nothing prissy or withheld about Jane, but I restrained myself. I asked her out on Friday night and she said, "Sure." Placid. No girlish coquetry or effusiveness.

I made the mistake of choosing *Ordinary People* for our first date. The wrong movie can fuck up everything in a new romance. Afterwards we went to a deli, not talking on the short drive. I was afraid that Jane's pensiveness indicated that she was impressed by the movie, and I didn't risk any wisecracks.

When we were seated at the deli, Jane's eyes flashed at me and she finally spoke: "If I never hear Pachelbel's godawful *Canon* again, I'll be happy. And if I never see poor Mary Tyler Moore play a frigid bitch again, I'll be even happier."

I smiled a wide smile of relief and bliss. Jane and I were going to get along.

MAKING JANE
HAPPY

----

*O*mar yanked me out of bed at nine A.M. by stuffing his dirty clothes in the hallway hamper. He slammed his boots on the floor of his room. He brushed his choppers with the bathroom door open and spat explosively. Each consecutive jolt of noise woke me up a little more. I had a painful piss hard-on. I rolled over. The needle scraped down on the Sex Pistols' *Great Rock 'N' Roll Swindle* album, with the volume cranked to eight.

I got up and limped to my private commode to pee. I put my robe on and went out and set the volume back to five. I went into the john, rinsed Omar's gob of peppermint spittle down the sink, and shaved. I let a cool shower drill me awake.

Omar was eating two runny fried eggs (spatulaed in thirds) on a hot-dog bun, microwaved tater tots, and hot chocolate with marshmallow plankton.

"Kevin's mom boot your ass out without givin' you breakfast?"

"Fuckin' Shredded Wheat..."

"This is just a brotherly suggestion—try eating a PG-rated meal once in a while. You got any idea what chewed-up eggs and cocoa looks like?"

"Fuck off."

I turned on the coffee and when it was hot poured myself a mug and sat opposite Omar and swilled it. Breakfast *chez* Carew.

Omar burrowed his schnozz into his mug to get at the marshmallow stuck to the sides. "Omar, Jane's coming over at one o'clock. Here's what I suggest you do. Listen now. I'm going to give you five bucks. By 12:45 I wanna see your ass *vanished.* There's a new Chuck Norris movie at the mall and it starts at 1:15. I give it my highest recommendation. After the movie, you can take a long, lingering stroll in the mall. Watch the pretty colored water in the fountain. Torment the poor clerk in the record store, see if he has the Germs in stock. Do some shoplifting. Whatever. I'll see that Dewey bails you out before sundown. Under no circumstances are you to return to this house before six o'clock. Got me?"

He guffawed. "Pretty nifty speech. Here's my counter-demands...I want ten bucks. Chuck Norris can bend over and wedge his head up his own ass for all I care. I'll go practice at Jack's house. But I need moola for chips and licorice and Mountain Dew. Five won't cover it at today's prices. I *might* drop in around four o'clock to check my mail and make a couple phone calls. Those are my final terms."

I got my second cup of coffee. "Omar, some day you'll mature and you'll look back on your adolescence with sorrow. You'll regret what you put your loved ones through... I'll give you five bucks and *loan* you the other five. I want that five back tomorrow. This is non-negotiable."

"Listen to Clarence Darrow here. There's a fart-mark on my shorts that you can kiss. Just to pity you I'll promise to stay away till four. You can't possibly screw for more than three hours. *I'll* loan *you* five when Dewey gives me my allowance tomorrow. Pay me back in seven days with a buck interest and we'll be square."

The Sex Pistols record came to the end of side one. Without the bellowing my mind went blank. "All right." I went to my room and got a five and five singles. I might end up working at 7-Eleven just to keep Omar at bay.

I went outside to water the [34] flower beds and I saw Omar pedaling up the street with Sam in pursuit a few minutes later. Bonnie came over with a plate of brownies and I made a fresh pot of coffee. We sat in the breezeway and had brunch.

"Ever read any Canadian fiction, Bud?"

"Ah, let's see...I read that Leonard Cohen novel about the nymphomanic Indian girl or whatever she was. And I read *The Apprenticeship of Duddy Kravitz* by Mordecai Richler. I like that one a lot."

"I haven't read those. I did see the movie of *Duddy Kravitz* on TV. I just finished reading *Fifth-Business* by Robertson Davies. Very good book. This guy's no hick Canuck. I'll bring it over next time."

"Is that the one about magicians? I think Jane read it."

"It's got some magic in it."

"Canadian movies do tend to bite weenie except for *Duddy Kravitz.* They did a good job on that one. Richard Dreyfuss was a riot when he rushed up and grabbed that film-lecturer around the leg. That was Duddy in a nutshell—just grab it."

Bonnie left at 12:30. I put clean sheets on my bed and got down at floor level and checked the slats. Jane and I had collapsed the bed a year ago. I brushed the chocolate out of my teeth and flossed. I put a touch of Dewey's cologne in my pits and on my belly. Bedazzle Jane with a new scent.

I sat on the couch and read the last couple pages of "Everything That Rises Must Converge" and exactly as I finished the story, my heart rising, Jane's bike whizzed into the driveway.

I met her at the door. We kissed. Jane had on a long-sleeved red-and-white striped cotton jersey and tight white shorts. I could smell suntan lotion, sun-warmed hair and clean skin. Instantly intoxicating. I got her a Dr Pepper and she drank it rapidly and belched.

One of the things I loved about Jane was her easy acceptance of stomach gurgles, burps and other spontaneous body noises. You could eat a salami, provolone and hot-pepper sandwich with her and not worry about the ramifications. Not even Omar's farting fazed her.

We went to my bedroom. I had two pink roses, slightly imperfect where Japanese beetles had gnawed them, in a water glass on the bed table. I had vacuumed the floor and swabbed all the wooden surfaces the day before.

I was already naked except for my cutoff jeans. I shucked them off and pitched them on the chair and then wriggled under the sheet to watch Jane.

Jane sniffed the roses. She walked over to my bookcase and browsed. She turned and smiled wanly. "You got your work cut out today, Bud. I felt really horny last night, but now I just feel blah."

"Hell. Get in here and let me try some of my hoodoo and voodoo, Miz Jane."

She slid off her jersey and undid her bra, keeping her back to me. She stepped out of her shoes—I saw polish on her toenails. I might go berserk and suck those little piggies later. She swiveled as she peeled her shorts off. She was wearing black-and-crimson panties that had F-R-I-D-A-Y stitched across the rump. "Ta-da..." She slipped into bed. "Just kidding, Bud. I'm so wet I'm starting to ooze..."

I got my hands inside her panties and eased them off as Jane lifted her legs to help. I tossed them on the chair. "I'm goin' south to check out this ooze situation," I said. I kissed Jane's lips, her neck, her nipples, her long smooth tan belly, and buried my face in her muff. I licked and teased her wet pussy avidly. I caressed her breasts at the same time and felt her hands tugging at my unruly hair (French anarchist hair, she called it). Five minutes, ten, fifteen—I loved oral sex as much as Quasimodo loved bells.

When I rose up and prepared to mount Jane, I had a strand of syrup hanging from my dick to my kneecap. My dick was the color of rhubarb.

Jane was shuddering, her nipples hard, her face flushed with color. She opened her eyes. "You gooey devil, you got a trapeze swinging from your thingamabob."

"That's no thingamabob, that's a dick. Let me show you."

I eased into her and felt ripples of sensation throughout my body. All that nonsense about male pleasure being localized in the dick! Not with Jane, it wasn't. My *feet* felt great when I was inside her.

I made love as slowly and steadily as I could, Jane's legs wrapped around me, beveling gently. Jane's hips and pelvis knew dance steps that I was still learning. If they taught these steps at the Arthur Murray schools, there'd be lines around the block waiting to register. Just when the sensation was peaking, she jogged me up another notch. Her fingers kneaded my shoulders. She yelped. Coming inside Jane was always a transfiguration—I burst out of my clumsy animal self and into my divine self. My heart and body were filled with joy at the apex of sensation and emotion.

No talk for a long time. We were like twin babies, happily moist, dawdling and cooing in a playpen. I held Jane at the waist, feeling the smooth inturned shape of her center, flesh and bone. I moved my palm dreamily over her lower back. Then both hands down onto her buttocks, shaping their firm plumpness. When I caught my breath at last, I kissed her and she accepted the taste of herself without finickiness. I stroked her hair, damp at the temples. I stroked her eyebrows and her cheeks, which were still flushed with erotic heat. I traced the soft incurve where her lips met, and she opened her mouth and nibbled my finger.

About three o'clock I went out and got us two big tumblers of ice water. The sheets were sopped. It was eighty degrees but not too muggy. O.T. revved up the lawnmower next door and the buzz of it encapsulated us. We didn't talk. Just drank our water, then kissed some more with cooler lips.

Jane's temple was dry now. "Let's go see *Local Hero* tomorrow night, sweetheart. Tony and I saw it Wednesday and it's a beauty."

"Good. I haven't seen a decent movie in months. What's the one where the woman pees in the cemetery?"

"*Smash Palace.*"

"That's the last good one I saw."

37

The front door clattered—Omar. I heard the refrigerator open and then the kitchen cupboard. Goddamn that little shitweasel. My door didn't lock, but I got up and crammed my desk chair under the doorknob. Jane was giggling.

Omar stalked up the hallway and stopped between his room and mine and sadistically stayed silent for a minute.

"Get the hell outta here, Omar. And you owe me ten bucks for shystering out of our deal."

"Deals, huh," Jane said. "You should know better, Bud. Omar's like the PLO—no deals."

Omar cut a fart. "It's growing, it's spreading, it's coming under the door. If I light a match, the house'll explode. Run for your lives, you fuckers…"

"Leave the house *now,* Omar!"

"You're too weak to make me, Bud Crud." He farted again. "Ahhh, that felt good. I'll huff 'n' I'll puff 'n' I'll blow your door down. Demolition room service—I got some graham crackers and grape jelly for you poontangers. C'mon, let me in."

He jiggled the knob. I shot out of bed and skinned my cutoffs on. I yanked open the door, spilling the chair aside, and my foot scraped a sticky surface as I stepped into the hall. Jellyfoot. Omar barreled up the hallway and through the breezeway. He was on his bike when I hit the hot pavement. The combination of jelly on my heel and the baked asphalt cost me traction. Omar sped away, honking his *ah-woo-gah* horn. Sam dashed at him and he gave the cur a left-footed kick in the chops. Sam retreated.

Given the circumstances, how severe could the penalty be for fratricide? A heavy fine at worst. Some community service, calling bingo games for shut-ins or stabbing trash on the interstate median. They'd never slap me behind bars.

If You've Never Been Fucked on a Saturday Night, You've Never Been Fucked at All

Saturday was a big day at Dewey's store, and everybody was in high spirits—Charles was in love, Penny was set to take a three-day holiday, I was seeing Jane later, Dewey had the latest *Penthouse* and a bottle of Rhine wine at home, and Omar and the Butt-Stabbers were poised on the lip of infamy (their debut was at the teen rec center at eight o'clock).

Omar put *The Misfits Walk Among Us* on the turntable and had us all groaning by 9:55. Dewey booted him out when the store opened and bribed him with five bucks for a second breakfast. By 10:30 the kids with the multicolored hair arrived in droves. Also, the Robert Smith and Siouxsie Sioux lookalikes. Their parents probably owned $300,000 houses in the Heights and worried themselves to a nub devising variants of "Where did we go wrong?" These kids were no more dangerous than I was when I went through my Joe Strummer phase circa 1980. To me the Ozzy Osbourne and Brian Johnson idolators were a lot scarier. We got a fair number of those, too—many carrying their motorcycle helmets and flexing their paws in fingerless leather gloves.

Mingling with the Brit-ghouls, Brit-mopes and heavy metal studs were generic New Wavers in loose shirts and jeans and baby boomers searching for those beloved Young Rascals or Procol Harum or Crosby, Stills & Nash (ugh) albums. Dewey tried to stock everything, and damn near everybody left happy.

From 12:30 to 3:00 I did my stint behind the register, and the mob of customers never seemed to thin out. The occasional R.E.M., Black Flag or Pere Ubu sale kept me from getting too ornery. Dewey had cautioned me to maintain my cool when some dunce purchased a stack of Pat Benatar or Kansas or Iron Maiden. Sometimes the ultra-judgmental jerk in me popped out and my politeness fizzled.

At 3:15, when business tapered a little, I sat with Penny in the office and split a pint of sorbet with her. I chipped out my half into Dewey's Slurpee cup.

Dewey had a triptych of enlarged photos on the desk: himself dressed as an Elvis impersonator; me at the mike, squalling away with my high school band, the December Boys; and Omar, busking at the mall, nose to nose with an Orange Julius clerk protesting his choice of repertoire—I think it was the Dead Kennedys' "Let's Lynch the Landlord."

Penny gazed at me and spooned a chunk of sorbet between her lips. "Well, Mr. Smugness Rising, I hope you appreciate your situation."

"Explain it to me, oh wise feminine one."

"Having Dewey for an uncle. Only having to work about ten hours a week. Having Jane for a squeeze."

"What's this 'squeeze' shit. If I said that, I'd have to hold my hands over my nuts, the attacks would come so fast and furious...Bud lubs Jane. All there is to it. Besides, I got Omar for a fifty-pound rotten albatross around my neck."

"He keeps things lively."

"Spoken by someone who's never lived in the same house with him. Omar thinks you're cool. You took him to see *Rock 'N' Roll High School* that one time, so you're an ally."

"I bet I could babysit him and have him eating out of my hand."

"You're deluded. He'd eat your *hand,* Penny. Omar makes Johnny Rotten look like Johnny Mathis."

"I could babysit Johnny Rotten, too."

The sorbet was making my teeth hurt. I finished the last spoonful and squirted some of Dewey's industrial-strength coffee into the cup and had a caffeine boost. It was actually a disgusto hot milkshake, mixed with the melted sorbet.

"I admire your bravado, Penny. You should ascend higher in life than assistant manager of a record store."

Penny took a drag on her cherry cigarillo. The smoke was like fumes from a fire in a cherry jam warehouse. "If we can swing the finances, Charles and I might buy Dewey out. We'll definitely can your ass as our first official act as new owners."

"Good. Dewey and I can both retire. Or we can manage Omar's career."

"Brian Epstein delusions, I see."

I had no comeback, so I got up and peeked out into the shop. There was an attractive blonde leafing through the S bins. Dewey refused to organize his stock in the standark rock-metal-r&b-reggae-folk-jazz-easy listening subcategories. She could be looking at Simon & Garfunkel or Shoes or Slade or Sly and the Family Stone.

"Excuse me," I said. I snuck out and browsed in the T's, admiring those quirky Talking Heads jackets and marvelling at how many Tangerine Dream albums existed. I eyed the blonde stealthily. She had short hair, which I usually disliked, but it looked good on her. She looked like a smart, quarrelsome edition of Goldie Hawn. Her tan legs and crisp tennis whites and big frost-blue eyes gave her an allure for sure.

I skipped over the Supremes and Sylvester (Dewey was a real card in stocking old disco) and edged next to her at Supertramp.

"Can I help you find something?" I asked brightly.

"Where's the Suicide?"

My gummy mental wheels spun for about five seconds before I comprehended her curt question. "They're probably holed up in New York City, eating cold beans and shooting rats with zipguns."

"Pretty funny." She didn't show even the slightest crinkle of a smile. She crossed her arms and gave me a cross, ÜberGoldie look.

"We've had them from time to time. But they're getting rare. People hang on to their copies religiously, I guess."

"So your ad is just bullcrap. You don't stock everything."

"All ads are bullcrap, ma'am." I winced at what wrath "ma'am" might trigger. At the same time I was eager to see what reaction she'd throw. I looked her right in her freezing pale-blue eyes and smiled my agreeable hippie smile.

"Well, mister clerk, I find your cynicism a total drag. You've lost a potential customer."

"A thousand apologies, Mama-San. Try some Styx. They got some pretty heavy albums, too." I bowed slightly and 41 walked away, my heart pattering. A harsh woman could knock me into an emotional tizzy. Being a shit was my best defense.

This blonde had killer aplomb. She backtracked from R all the way to ABBA, spending forty-five minutes before she left, her clockwork ass sashaying out the door at 4:30.

"Gave you a boner, too, huh?" Charles said. Charles had a healthy, athletic body, but he wore atrocious clothes, Coke-bottle glasses and Salvation Army boondockers. He had a bad crop of hair, too. His dome looked like a muddy bird's nest with a freckled egg in it.

"Kinda. That could be a real bad-vibes fuck, though."

"Kinda! A boner's a boner. Try 'em all, Bud. The mean ones'll surprise you."

"Is that what you're into these days?"

"Nah. Well—partially. Lydia's not easy to categorize. Haven't quite figured her out yet."

"Bring her to the picnic on the fourth so I can check her out."

"I might."

"Penny's bringing her mystery man. We can have a wet T-shirt contest and talent show."

"Lydia'd win."

"She got whoppers?"

"They're not small."

"Big tits are overrated. Strictly novelty value." I was joshing him. I'd never dated a girl who was really buxom—just Cissie at Athens with her friendly mooshy sideways-sloping sloppy tits that were more *unleashed* than big. The possibility of fondling, kissing, and sucking big tits awed me and even scared me some. What the hell—I loved Jane, and her beautiful perfect small breasts.

"You'll change your tune. Don't get too complacent. I see big ones on the horizon for you."

I crossed my eyes. "On the horizon, huh? Is this like *The Boobs from 50,000 Fathoms?* Hope they don't squash me."

Dewey saved me from my imaginary breastaphobia. He gave me some boxes of tapes to put in the cases. At 6:30 he moseyed over and took out his wallet.

"Here's twenty, Bud. Go home and eat and relax awhile before you go out. Charles can give me a ride later."

"Thanks, Dew. Actually, Omar owes me ten. If you could take it off his allowance, I'd be grateful."

"He'll throw a fit. I'll advance you ten, and you can work it out with Omar later."

"That's fine."

Dewey was a pacifist and I respected his don't-antagonize-Omar policy. I drove home and showered and ate a can of chicken gumbo soup and watched part of the Cubs game on cable. Harry Carey was fulminating enjoyably. I left at twilight to pick up Jane.

When I arrived, Freddie was sitting on the front porch and feeding saltines to his malamute, Mandingo—a 150-pound black-and-silver bruiser with a raccoon-mask face. When he saw me coming up the walk, Freddie barked, "Kill, Mandingo! Kill the hippie!"

"Hey Freddie."

"Jane's not ready. I think she's upstairs burning a wart off her ass."

"I like you, Fred."

"You won't like me for long. Mom's gonna take Jane to the pussy-doctor next week and if it turns out she's not a virgin—zowie! I get t'hunt you with my bow. Ever see *Deliverance?*"

"Yeah, I did, Fred. Those backwoods bad boys are your role model, huh?"

Mandingo swiped a paw at Freddie, coaxing another cracker.

Jane came through the door, dressed in a blue skirt and white

43

blouse like a stewardess. What an airline that would be—boners raised from coast to coast.

"Let Mandingo feed you for a change, Freddie." She pinched him on the shoulder.

"You're all gonna die," stentorian Freddie said.

"Hey Fred," I said. "You diddle around on the guitar a little, doncha? I'll ask Omar t'give ya an audition."

"I wouldn't go within fifty yards of that fuckwad."

I shrugged. "You're passing up your only chance at glory."

"*Friday the 13th in 3-D* is the one to see."

"Why don't parents quit after one kid," I said to Jane as we got into the car.

"They were trying for another me." She goosed me.

After the movie, I felt horny and tender. I sat in the parking lot while headlights raked us and kissed Jane. I honked the horn when I squirmed to give my hard-on some extra space to nose around in.

"Well, we can't go to Scotland, but we can go to Pam's," Jane said.

Jane's friend Pam was house-sitting for her vacationing parents and perchance could lend us a bedroom. Neither Jane nor I could regress to outdoor or backseat fucking after experiencing the luxury of a bed. We were spoiled white brats.

Pam had her hair in curlers and a greenish mudpack on her face, but she was good humored about the intrusion. She sat on the sofa, eating miniature Reese's peanut-butter cups and watching a horror movie on TV as we climbed the stairs.

Pam's bed was a flophouse for stuffed animals and her tortoise-shell cat Bunky (who was only marginally more alive than the teddy bears). Jane set Bunky in the hall and closed the door, as I evicted the stuffed bears.

"Tony says that too many stuffed animals on a girl's bed is an ominous sign."

"How many is too many?"

"Any number higher than zero."

Jane made a comic sneer. "You guys. Tony's likely never been in a girl's bedroom."

"You're wrong about that. I know of at least two shell-shocked young honeys."

"He couldn't get laid at a nymphomaniacs' convention."

I laughed. "You been hanging out in pool-halls again?"

"I play snooker now and then."

"You know what's worse than stuffed animals? A copy of *Jonathan Livingston Seagull* on the bed."

Jane let me undress her. With my heart knocking I undid the tight-loop button at her neckline and reaching around her thumbed open the descending row of buttons. I felt her bare warm tummy.

"Your hands are sweaty, mister."

"Hot night. Every'thin' g'wan be sweaty soon, Miz Jane."

I unzipped her skirt and palmed her silk-clad ass. I was too excited and twitchy to continue. As Jane shed her bra and panties, I scrambled out of my ratty duds like a spastic fire drill. I could smell Pam's cosmetics and clothes. I vaulted onto the bed and embraced Jane.

In the warm equatorial evening air, on the strange soft-mattressed bed, we kissed. A halo of blue-white street light hung in the upper corner of the window. A soft amber bed light lit the dark button-eyed bears, jammed into a phalanx on the chair, watching us. I was in a kissing-licking-slurping frenzy, and Jane's body was nature's sweetest organic lapstuff. I licked my way to her pussy: sweet-tart, meat-and-fish-and-ambrosia lovepie. Nothing else on earth or anywhere else in the galaxy tasted better.

We turned Pam's bed into a slippery bog, and lay there in the slightly cooling A.M. air, kissing and stroking and communicating in our fluent nonverbal post-fuck murmurs. Bunky pawed at the bottom of the door, but we wouldn't let him in.

At 1:30 we got dressed dreamily and went downstairs.

"Whatcha watchin', sleepyhead?" Jane asked. She put her hands on Pam's shoulders and peered at the murky TV image.

"It's called *Year 2889*. They scraped the bottom on this one. I'm ready to hit the hay. I hope you guys are satiated."

"We are," I said. "Hope you got some dry sheets handy, Pammie. Things are a little moist in there...What's that monster got for eyes? Ping-Pong balls?"

Pam sighed. She didn't look bad minus the curlers and mudpack. "I got the sheet angle covered...He's a cave monster. He's got those underground cave orbs."

"I wish we could stay and see the end of this...Thanks for the flop, Pammie. Our apologies to the cat. I'll fix you up with Zak as a return favor. He speaks very fondly of you."

Pam stretched a leg and turned the TV off with her big toe. "Bud, shitcan the comedy. Take him away, Jane."

We all said good night. Nobody had liked my jokes today.

HOT SABBATH

*I*t was gruesomely hot on Sunday, and Jane was off for an enforced three-day visit to her grandparents in Sandusky. I imagined her trapped in the car with Freddie and Mandingo, then lazing around her grandparents' mansion that smelled of apple butter and dust. Their 1001 knickknacks, their puce ottoman, their framed prints of ostriches and goony birds, their massive bookcase full of Reader's Digest Condensed Books. Seventy-two hours of morbid boredom, eating creamed vegetables, listening to Sir Edward Elgar records, and reading *Marjorie Morningstar*—the condensed but still overlong version.

In the afternoon Dewey set up the badminton net and finagled Omar into playing. Except for pro wrestling and demolition derby, Omar disdained sports. The only time I ever saw Dewey threaten him with corporal punishment was when Omar called Brian Sipe a pussy.

When Kevin wandered into the yard, his narrow dogface sweaty from the trip over, Dewey and I played doubles against the adolescent snots. Omar's strategy was to blurt a fart just as Dewey was serving and make him fault. It worked about half the time.

It was too hot to cook anything. Around seven o'clock Kevin and Omar ate some rice cakes smeared with peanut butter and jam. Dewey whipped up a blender of margaritas, and we sat light-headed in the breezeless evening, drinking and blinking the bugs away.

"You guys alive over there?" Bonnie yelled from her backyard. She was wearing bright-orange shorts, her thighs bursting out of them like tree trunks.

"We drink, therefore we exist," Dewey yelled back.

Bonnie trundled over to the edge of our yard. "*Pat Garrett and Billy the Kid* is on the late show, Bud," she told me.

Bonnie knew that I idolized Sam Peckinpah, but much of *Pat Garrett* was spoiled by Kris Kristofferson's numbnuts portrayal of Billy.

Dewey nominated me to make a second pitcher of margaritas, and Bonnie had one with us. The bug-zappers were sizzling some of the mosquitoes and gnats, but plenty of bugs flew lower and kamikazed us. Cleveland must be God's favorite bug experiment.

Dewey gave Omar fifteen bucks, and he and Kevin hiked to the Sub Shop to get four large roast-beef subs. Our heads were starting to buzz from the combination of alcohol and hunger. We went inside and turned on the fans. We couldn't decide what music to play—Dewey wanted The Isley Brothers, I was in a NRBQ mood—so we left the stereo off.

The phone rang and I answered.   "I have a long-distance collect call

47

from Greensward, Oregon, for a Mister Bud Carew or a Mister Omar Carew. Will you accept the charges?"

"Yeah." It was Mom.

"Who's there?" A giddy, scratchy voice. Mom was American, Ohio born, but she sounded like the British actress Sarah Miles.

"It's me. Bud. How are you, Mom?"

"Bud! I'll pay for this, I promise. I just don't want Hano to see the bill. I've been getting all these negativity points lately and I'm kind of—*besmirched.* Telephones are on the negativity list. They're two-pointers."

"I bet that's a long list. How come he has a phone on the property? Or did he get it consecrated by the phone-shaman?"

"Oh Bud! He has his business affairs. You know. Hano's not *punitive.* He's not one of these cartoon demigods or whatever. He's a terribly complicated man."

"Who keeps track of all this negativity stuff? Conan the scorekeeper?"

"Honey, stop it. We don't even have a fence around the property up here. Fishermen and hikers walk right in and they're *welcome.* It's totally benign."

"Mom, I hope you ain't been brainwashed. But what the hell—if you're happy..."

"I *am* happy. Sort of. It's so difficult to explain—your dad...We have animals. Bud—we've got a sea lion in a special saltwater pool. Hear him?"

I *could* hear a distant honking commotion like Harpo Marx on a faraway TV, along with the crackling in the connection and Mom's emotional gasps and gurgles. Mom was always simmering like a stovepot with feeling.

"What've you been up to, Mom?"

"Oh—weaving rugs. Working in the orchard. Planting our gardens. We had some terrible frost in late April. Oh! You know what I saw in the community room the other night, Bud?"

"What? Bigfoot?"

"No, on TV…It was Omar in a *Pink Panther* movie. He was so adorable playing the villain…"

My little brother was named for Omar Sharif—my mom's favorite movie at the time of his birth was *Doctor Zhivago.* I was named for her previous pet romantic epic—*Splendor in the Grass,* specifically the poon-chaser that Warren Beatty played therein. When my dad was drunk or sportive, he called us Yuri and Warren. He always referred to Mom's favorite flicks as *Doctor Cow-Eyes* and *Splendor up Her Ass* as Mom, flustered, whammed him on the biceps. My dad was a wiseguy, not really malicious or bullying. His favorite movies were more on the order of *Kiss Me Deadly* and *The Big Sleep.*

"I missed that one, Mom."

"He plays bridge, you know."

There was a whooshing desperation in that simple phrase. "Mom—are you doing all right?" I was starting to sweat and Dewey aimed a fan in my direction. Omar and Kevin barged in with the food.

"I'm fine! No meat, no eggs, no butter. I weigh one-ten. You should see me."

"I'd like to, Mom. I'd like to check your eyes with a penlight just to make sure old Hano hasn't done a number on you. It's hard for me not to picture this commune deal as *Night of the Living Vegetable Choppers*…I hate to do it to you, Mom, but Omar's here, and I'm gonna let you talk to him." The famished brat was unwrapping his sandwich. "I'm sorry if I teased you too much. You know I love you…Here he is." I pressed the phone to Omar's noggin and he swatted me. He took the phone with a bush-pig grunt.

"Hey Ma… no… eatin' dinner, tryin' to… yeah… nah, that's okay… mostly Cs and a D in gym 'cause I cussed the pushead teacher… no, they wouldn't dare… yeah… yeah, tenth… he's okay for an old creep… he beats me with a strap once in a while… nah, just kidding… yeah… not this year, I got my new band goin'… okay, here he is…"

49

Omar passed the phone to Dewey, who was lathering mayo on his hoagie. "Lorelei, you heartbreaker...what? they're both okay, don't panic...Bud's fine, he's educated now at least...don't worry about money...of course I do, I think about Roy every day, but I don't *mourn* anymore...well, we differ on that... Roy had a wild life, a marathon...I might live to be eighty, I might die tomorrow, I don't *worry* about it...Mortality's got us all buffaloed, Lorelei...Cry a little, sweetheart, it'll make you feel better...yeah, Omar's gonna support me in my dotage, that's the only reason I put up with his nonsense...don't throw ashtrays, Omar...slow down, Lorelei, you got three sentences going at once...he won't come up there, I tried to talk him into it, too...whoah...all right...here he is..."

Dewey wiped sweat off his brow and handed me the phone. I had a big bite of sandwich in my mouth.

"Bud, tell Omar he has to visit in July or August. No excuses. Dewey's too—too *malleable.* You do it now. I'm counting on seeing you both. I hate myself for missing your graduation. You can fly out and see me in September yourself."

"Ah, Mom. I'll be glad to come see you as long as I can bring my independent fact-finding team. I wanna grill this Hano guy. But you know I can't get Omar to do anything. I couldn't talk him into picking up a dirty sock."

"Yes you can. Omar will listen if you're sincerely brotherly. I have to hang up now. Let me know what the bill comes to. It's singalong time in the community room."

"Doin' a lot of Led Zeppelin up there?"

"Quit teasing me, Bud. You're so much like—you call me after you convince Omar. I love you both. Dewey too. I wish I could touch you all. My hands are quivering. My whole body is..."

A deep blush of emotion reddened my face. I could feel Mom ache. "We love you, too, Mom. Sorry about the teasing. Bye."

"Wait!"

"What?"

50

"Play some ball with Omar, Bud. He needs to get his gym grade up."

"Mom, Christ and Gandhi and Malcolm X in tandem couldn't get Omar to play ball. Trust me. The kid don't—like—balls. He might play Wiffle ball with Joey Ramone, but I even doubt that."

"You try."

"Okay. You go sing before you get more demerits. Bye." I hung up.

"Talking to Lorelei's better than a Tennessee Williams play, eh *kemosabe?*" Dewey said and winked at me.

I scratched my hair and sighed. I didn't begin to understand my mom. She was passionate yet conscientious, intelligent yet ditzy, solid in her beliefs yet infinitely suggestible. In repose—if you could ever capture her in repose—she was a beautiful forty-three-year-old widow with a heart-shaped face, brown eyes, and thick curly brown hair like mine. Yet she was a wreck. A thousand hours of meditation couldn't subtract an iota of her anxiety.

The crew in our living room had simpler problems. Kevin's face was a mayonnaise-and-shredded-lettuce catastrophe—his vehement chewing style shot debris onto his kisser like a scythe dicing weeds. Omar had finished his twelve-incher and was swiping the other half of Dewey's. Carrying my sandwich with me to protect it, I went into the kitchen and blasted up another blender of margaritas.

"It's a tossup which is worse," Dewey said. "The heartburn these things give you or the headache you get when you drink too many of 'em."

"The trick is to eat a lot of chips and salsa with 'em, so it all evens out in your stomach and harmonizes."

Omar turned on MTV—another torture device to nettle twentieth-century image-addicts. Some mop-headed bastard was explaining the dry-ice intricacies of a spent video.

"Where the hell's the babes? Who's this turdface?" Omar bitched.

"Yowza. I'd take the blonde over the brunette," Kevin said.

"I'd do 'em both," Omar said.

Dewey chuckled. "What's it comin' to, Bud? Even the virgins are jaded swingers. How 'bout you? I'm partial to Martha myself."

"Yeah. She's a little skinny, but she's got those big bright slip-me-the-dick eyes. I forget what the blonde looks like. Is it that raggedy dishpan one with the nervous twitches? Kind of a Sally Struthers deal? I'd have to think twice about taking her to the sack."

"Bigger knockers than plain Jane. She's got the flat ones, not the fat ones."

"Omar, since I'm on orders to play ball with you, I think I'll use your head for a kickball. That blonde's got half Jane's I.Q., one-tenth of her personality, and one-twentieth of her beauty."

Culture Club appeared on screen and Omar hiked down his shorts and mooned Boy George.

"Cram your butt back in your diaper, Omar," Dewey said. "There's nothing more unsightly than a bare-assed white boy."

"Who says I'm white?" He farted.

Dewey fanned himself with a newspaper.

"Hey ass-blast, you're going to see Mom this summer and that's final," I said.

"Only if you kill me first and send me in a coffin. I'm not eatin' that orange and apple and coconut shit." He meant the communal fruit salad.

"We'll put some sliders from White Castle on ice for you," Dewey said mildly.

"You're hallucinatin' if you think I'm gonna go...Look at these twatheads!" The band called A Flock of Seagulls came whirling on the screen. I swooned at the dodgem-cart camera-work, the nightmare hairdos, the calliope-jingle-from-outer-space music.

"They don't sound as bad as they look," Dewey said.

"What would Elvis think?" I said.

"He'd shoot the screen out."

Omar found a bowl of custard in the refrigerator and challenged Kevin to a custard speed-eating contest. Dewey and I topped off our margarita glasses and retired to the breezeway, where it was cooler now.

"Sunday, bloody Sunday," I said.

"What ever happened to Glenda Jackson?"

"Wasn't she in that movie about the poet that we went to see—*Stevie?*"

"Oh yeah. That was years ago, though. I remember her more spooking the cows in *Women in Love.* Glenda was a load—like your mom."

"Mom isn't hard-bitten like Glenda."

"Yeah, but she's still a load. I warned Roy when he met her. She's pretty, she's vivacious, but she ain't exactly feathers. She's a *load.*"

I shook my head and took a slug of sour citrus-tasting margarita. I probably put too much lime juice in the damn things. I think bartenders usually sweeten them with sugar. We'd both have to swig some Pepto later.

WEDNESDAY,
HORNY
WEDNESDAY

I subbed for Penny on Monday and Tuesday and sublimated at night. Sweet torment, but no touching. I slapped my hand away from my engorged dick. I pictured the pretty marine biologist and the hotel-keeper's sexy wife in *Local Hero,* then Jane in white-silk panties and bra (her taut skin, her legs around me, her hips mamboing me to ecstasy). Then Debra Winger in *Urban Cowboy.* Oww. If you laid all the boners raised by that actress end to end, you'd have a monorail to Mars.

I got up to get a Dr Pepper and   sat in the kitchen and paged through an old *Rolling Stone* with a big coffee stain on Bill Murray's face on the cover. Omar had drawn mustaches and tusks and goiters on most of the inner illustrations.

The birds started chirping outside and I decided to take a walk in the dawn. The lawn was wet with dew. Bob Steingruber's tired-ass old Olds was parked in his driveway, the dew turning its layer of road dust to mud.

Sam scrambled across his yard and tagged along with me, panting and grinning and pissing a squirt every ten feet. He didn't assault pedestrians, only vehicles. I walked the seven blocks to Mayfield Road and watched the sun light the trees and buildings to the east. Sam cut across a church parking lot and paused to whiz on the shrubbery near the sermon-board: ALL YE OF FAITH GATHER HERE. I walked seven more blocks to the donut shop and bought an apple fritter and another Dr Pepper. Too fucking hot for coffee.

The waitress gave me the weary fisheye: anyone buying a soda at six A.M. and paying with quarters and dimes dug out of dirty, lint-filled pockets was a potential serial killer. I considered a few cracks—"Boy, that Ted Bundy was a character" or "There hasn't been a really good donut-shop spree-killer in years, has there?" or "I can taste Satan in this fritter"—but I checked myself. My gags had been stiffing lately, and this old sourpuss might haul out a sawed-off pool cue and clobber me.

I walked home and read my Flannery O'Connor collection until Dewey got up at 8:30. Omar emerged bare chested in his pajama bottoms, his hair spiked out like a damp porcupine.

"I hate it when I go to take a piss and it comes out all sideways," he grumbled.

"Quit jerkin' off so much and that won't happen. You get your dick tip all clogged up like a glue bottle."

"Get a paper towel and swab the floor," Dewey said.

Omar ignored it, as he did all hygienic suggestions. He put two sausage patties in a frying pan. He dug his little finger around in his earholes, gouging at the wax. He hit the counter with a spatula and sang a little bit of "Surfin' Bird." He unwrapped two cinnamon Pop Tarts and jammed them into the toaster. He put some hash browns on a plate in the microwave. Beep. He flipflopped the charring sausage patties. Probably had the burner on HIGH. He knocked the greasy spatula on the stove, machine-gunning bird lyrics through his vibrating lips.

Dewey dodged the jiggling spatula and filled his coffee cup. He sat reading the box scores and rubbing his feet. I had my third Dr Pepper of the morning. I was on a jag.

In the breezeway I spread out on the chaise lounge and dozed until Dewey left for work. Omar followed him shortly, lugging his bass. The Butt-Stabbers' debut had attracted a cult following—fourteen unruly kids at the rec center. There was some damage to furniture and one window broken. Dewey paid the tab and docked Omar's allowance by half for three months.

At 11:00 Jane called, just as I was getting ready to dial her. "Bud, I got good news and bad news."

"What's the good?"

"Freddie's staying with my grandparents till Sunday."

"How fortuitous," I said, imitating Dewey imitating W. C. Fields. "What's the bad, lambpie?"

"Drop that voice thing or I'll ram something sharp into your kneecap when you get over here...The bad is not really bad, just nature's monthly trick— I got my period last night."

"Damn! I'm so horny I'm afraid I'll come through my nose if I sneeze."

"Tough luck."

"I'm not faint-hearted, baby. I've put bandages on my own cuts. I've seen George Romero movies. How gory can it be? Not much different than a shrimp cocktail with a little hot sauce. Yummy."

"You scuzzo! There goes that friendly, compassionate handjob I was gonna give you." Jane was chortling, though. She wouldn't abandon me in my hour of need.

"We'll figure something out. Love conquers just about everything...When's your mom leaving?"

"She's already gone. She gave me the third degree when you didn't come inside last Saturday."

"Baby, your mom would like to tie me to a chair and blowtorch the bottoms of my feet. She just won't admit it. It's hypocritical to say, 'Evenin', Miz Simmons. My, don't you look lovely in that Hawaiian frock. Aren't we havin' lovely weather?...'"

"Bud, remove your head from your ass. My mom doesn't own any Hawaiian frocks. She's always been civil. You're paranoid."

"Am not. She'd put a hit out on me if she wasn't chicken. I'm gonna fire over there and set your body straight. I'll work on your mind at a later date."

Jane scoffed. "If you ever took a really good crap, you'd disappear."

"Your anger be stirrin' my blood, Bess."

She hung up on me. I showered and shaved and added a splash from Dewey's cologne pot. I drove over to the hellish, tar-seething 7-Eleven lot and parked opposite the 15 MINUTE PARKING ONLY sign. I bought Jane an ice-cream sandwich as a peace, love & harmony offering. When I came scuffing up the walk, she was sitting on the porch petting Mandingo. White blouse and red shorts and bare feet with chipped toenail polish. I wanted to kiss her everything.

We kissed and I cuddled her as she bit open the cellophane and began to eat her melting ice-cream sandwich . "Want some?" I took a few licks. We had a cold-hot soul kiss going and I gripped Jane's hands. My blood was surging.

"Let's go upstairs so I can pledge my eternal love and devotion."

"Don't rush me, Jack." I put my head in her lap and she gave me a Dutch rub. "Let me feel." She plunged her hand into my shorts. "Gotcha."

Jane withdrew her hand and wiped it on my bare knee. "You can keep your own goop." She let Mandingo into the backyard and shut the gate. She gave him the last piece of ice-cream sandwich, which he inhaled. I followed her inside and she stopped to fuss with her hair in front of an ornate mirror. I squeezed her ass gently.

"Quit it." She knocked my wrist.

"My ass-grabbin' privileges are suspended until when? What'd I do? I needs to lubs you *now,* baby. My heart aches, my hair hurts, my shoes are too tight. Anything. Please. We could just neck and dry-hump. A tribute to the late seventies, sort of."

"I'd rather join a convent."

"This period thing is worse than I thought. Hey, I know I'm selfish, I'm insistent, I'm a pain in the butt, but I love you. Totally."

"Oh you poor little lamb. I just wish men could bleed out their ass once a month, then we'd be even."

I was stymied for an answer, so I kept quiet. We climbed the stairs. I felt exactly like a twenty-one-year-old knucklehead with no debating skills. I took Jane by the waist inside her room and turned her and kissed her. She came out of the kiss giggling.

"Relax, Bud. You're a fright when you're uptight."

I smiled. "Anything you say, Ms. Mood Swing."

Jane frowned. "There goes your chance at a blowjob. Why don't you jerk off and I'll watch. I wanna see you make monkey-faces and go 'Uh-uh-uh.' "

"Don't torture me, Jane."

"Oh you are a hopeless mess. No manual skills. Here." She unzipped my shorts and hauled me aloft. "A rocket. And it's leaking fuel. I bet I can make you come like a jackrabbit."

"Not if you browbeat me. I'm sensitive."

"Looks like a banana with a sunburn." Jane chuckled.

"Does not."

"Let's try this." She began to stroke me with both hands like a potter, her grin turning to a flush, her hair trailing over her merry eyes. "Here we go. Geronimo!"

I groaned and jism shot out of my high-hat boner and shot past Jane's fingers toward the ceiling. I'd never come so quick in my life.

Jane was laughing. "Banana went boom." She used a tissue to mop the bedspread and my still stiff dick. I groaned and came again into the wadded Kleenex.

"What the hell…"

"Love secrets of the Amazon," Jane said.

"Go on. That's bullshit. I just haven't come in three days. That stuff builds up."

Jane kissed me. We embraced and flopped back on the bed. She switched on her fan and the cool jetstream made her tendrils of hair part. I felt light-headed, bamboozled. Maybe that donut shop hag had slipped a mickey in my Dr Pepper. Essence of rapido ejaculato.

I took Jane's blouse and bra off and caressed her breasts. I could feel that she wanted to make love. "Let me touch you, Jane. Please. Just through your panties." I kissed her ear, nibbled. "Please."

"Quit begging. It's unseemly."

"I don't care what's seemly. Please let me touch your sweet pussy immediately or I'll collapse into a coma on this bed."

"One touch and it's all over."

"Aha. An admission on Miz Jane's part of horniness."

"Yeah, but it'll mess me up if I get started."

"Life is messy. Submit to it."

She knuckled my head. "I'm not getting through to you, Bud. I'm horny—but I'm also sluggish, I'm skittish, I feel off plumb. Can't we just kiss and hold each other? Or are you gonna be a beast?"

"Beast." I kissed Jane for about five minutes. My dick was still as hard as a metal pipe. "I'll eat you if you let me, sweetheart. Like in *Endless Love*—not the cheap-shit movie, the book. That's such a great scene."

"You and your great scenes. No wonder the high school library banned that book... If we crossed the English Channel in a storm, you'd reenact the upchuck scene from *Death on the Installment Plan*."

"Sure I would. It's the greatest upchuck scene ever written."

"It's certainly the most detailed."

"Céline knocks every other writer dizzy. I wanta go to Paris and lay some flowers on his grave."

"Wasn't he a Nazi?"

"No! He was just fucked up and confused. He had a plate in his head. He sounds like a Monty Python routine, but he was a great writer. He wasn't violent in real life."

"You should read five or six I. B. Singers to make up for grotty old Céline."

"I'm not an anti-Semite. My mother's half-Jewish for Christ's sake! And I've read *The Slave* and *Enemies: A Love Story*. They're wonderful books. Bernard Malamud, too. I've got Jews up the wazoo."

"Well, keep going. Do a penance. I'll loan you *The Spinoza of Market Street*."

"You're so good to me—dynamite handjobs, books, tips on ethnic tolerance, lunch even...Please let me eat you, baby..."

Jane yanked my nose. "You wanna leave this room with your nose still in the center of your face? I'll twist it. You're getting a chicken salad sandwich and a glass of iced tea. That's it."

"Fine with me. But I have to touch your sweet sore pussy just once. Just a pet. Or I'll die."

"You baby."

I held Jane's hands and leaned over her and kissed her and ran my toes along her ankle. I was still miserably hard. I fit myself between Jane's legs and pressed the crotch of her shorts. Just a touch. Yet when she pressed back and I felt her warmth,

I swooned and came in a flurry into the taut fabric. I was a hopeless Roman sperm-candle. Warm fingers, tissue, cotton fabric—anything that touched me made me ejaculate.

"Are you shooting for the record books, Bud?"

"Looks like I totaled your shorts. Sorry, baby."

"We're gonna have to get you a firearms permit. Three times in twenty minutes. Jeez!"

"It was actually three parts of one giant squirt. I need to be inside my natural habitat to get it right."

"Nope. Off limits."

"Know what? I still wanna eat you, baby."

"You're getting chicken salad and that's it."

Jane put on some Tobacco Road blue-jean cutoffs. What a knockout. I was ready to try for salvo number four. We went downstairs and had lunch and sat under the apple tree in the backyard and picked a few tiny green apples and fed them to Mandingo. He ate them like peanuts. Jane dropped a piece of sandwich into his wolf jaws. Crunch and gone.

I hate to admit it, but I still had an erection.

THE
SEPARATION
MANTRA

$\mathcal{D}$isaster struck Thursday morning—Jane phoned and said that she was leaving Saturday for the Cape. The dreaded family vacation. Five weeks of enforced celibacy. Omar would have to put a pick-a-number machine beside his *Penthouse* collection. Worse yet, Jane's awful parents were taking her out to dinner Thursday—celebrating the summer solstice with a House of Pancakes pigout. I could imagine Freddie chug-a-lugging every colored syrup on the lazy Susan, going into sugar shock, and raping a potted plant.

"Uhhhnnn…Listen, baby. Sneak over here Friday afternoon and we'll have an afternoon marathon. Omar won't be here. Uhhhnnn."

"Stop groaning, Bud. Jesus. I'll be back in August. We'll have a whole month before school starts. I'll make you come four times in an hour. I promise."

"I want that in writing tomorrow. The party of the first part, namely Miz Jane Simmons, does guaran-fuckin'-tee to satisfy the party of the second part, namely the hopeless erotomaniac Bud Carew, four, count 'em, four times in the space of sixty, count 'em, sixty minutes. If the aforesaid satisfaction is not reached, Mr. Carew demands that the terms be extended exponentially—namely, five, count 'em, five squirts in the space of one hour. Uhhhnnnn."

"What a goddamn baby. I can't believe you're twenty-one and still squalling like this." I could hear an exasperated fondness in Jane's tone. Otherwise I might've went apeshit with denial and self-pity. (She was right, of course. I *was* a terrible lovestruck baby.)

"Jane." Pause. Low chuckle from her end. "I love you."

"Yeah, yeah. I *almost* love you. Except when you make me feel like your wet nurse." Another chuckle.

"You said the magic word."

"What? 'Almost'? Aren't you pissed and insecure?"

"No, 'wet.' I love it that you're wet. That 'almost' is just temporary derangement. Get here by noon tomorrow and be prepared for frantic, last-ditch lovemaking. You'll never say 'almost' again."

"It'sa—gonna—be—messy."

"That's the way I want it. Remember *Endless Love.*"

"How could I forget it? Go put an icepack on your cock. I'll see you tomorrow."

I couldn't read, couldn't listen to music, couldn't do anything. I got on my bike and rode until I was winded. It was as muggy as a fat man's ass-crack in a steam bath. Dense gray clouds and burps of thunder. I sat in the park, watching the squirrels feud and fight and frig around. I considered a scheme: borrow dough from Dewey and tail Jane to Massachusetts. Using theatrical makeup and a suckass preppie voice, impersonate a suave jerk and wow Jane's parents. Oceanside cavorting to follow. My fake David Niven mustache coming loose in Jane's muff. Fried clams from a dilapidated clam shack and some heroic fucking on the beach at sundown. A dip in the briny sea and then use each other as human salt-licks all night long. My brain was a bubbling priapic cauldron.

Thunder rumbled closer as I mused in the darkening park. When did lust start to overrule everything else in my life? It must've been the first day of study hall—September, '75—when Miss Jalilah came click-clacking up the aisle on her high heels, patrolling for sleepers and note-passers and comic-book readers and all varieties of fuckoff. She was a tall, imperious brunette in a tight white dress, her ass perfectly round, her legs beautiful. Her stern expression made her even sexier. And her name—exotic, biblical and playmate-like all at once—was like a caress that made the hairs on my balls prickle. I sat there in a daze of tender lust. My dick arched up and out, and I squirmed for fifty minutes. When I got up to go to English class, it looked like I had egg white embedded in the fly of my light-gray slacks.

I fantasized endlessly about classmates—shy, blonde, milky-skinned Terri Allenson especially—and I melted mentally into Miss Jalilah a thousand times. I wanted to make her smile. My earliest dates were all slapstick, fumblings, pratfalls, strained chatter. It was lucky for me that some of those girls had a sense of humor. The punchline was usually "whoops." I didn't lose my virginity until my senior year, and the conditions were not ideal—barricaded by a pile of coats in a bedroom at a party, I entered plain, sweet, moaning, semi-drunk Janet Stotz and stroked like a baboon in a motion-sickness experiment, clumsily fondling whatever I could reach (mostly her shoulder-blades, which weren't as tactile as what I wanted to stroke), and came with a panicky jolt just as two girls, clucking like shocked hens, spread light on us as they fumbled for their lost parkas.

Meeting Jane was like entering the ideal imaginary country. It took a few months, but we learned how to kiss and touch and meld. With her there was no boundary between love and lust, no shame, no awkwardness, no picayune rules. I loved making love to her. I loved her insults and her dry mocking surface as much as I loved her endearments and her sensual abandon, her sopping wet pussy and the feel of her legs around me, her love-wrestling ardor.

I could remember the most intensely happy day of my life exactly—March 29, 1981. Jane and I were in bed for the first time and I had just had an orgasm, so strongly and ecstatically that I was a quivering, incoherent piece of happy flesh. I was still hard but outside her, and Jane pressed her thigh against my leg, moaning and yipping and babbling in extraterrestrial tongues, and rubbed herself to a chain of climaxes like firecrackers going off in slow motion. I watched her in wonder—the blush that colored her face, her strange cries, her unselfconscious pleasure as she came and came and came.

It was nothing that I did—I had no reliable skills as a lover yet. It was simply a matter of having privacy, time, passion and trust. With Jane I had a closeness and strength of feeling that overwhelmed me. I held her and stroked her and kissed her, and she continued to quiver liquidly and moan wordlessly. I thought that she might sob, she was so wiped out. But she finally sighed and made a coughing laugh and broke the wordless spell by saying, "God, that was a good one."

I laughed too. I gripped her hands and kissed her. Wriggling lower, I lay my face on her breasts. Jane stroked my head. We were in love for good at that moment. No matter how long the separations, no matter how taunting Jane got at her friskiest, no matter what obstacles were raised, we would always love each other.

The thunder had the squirrels in a tizzy. They stunt-walked along the high branches. They leapt acrobatically and darted down the trunk like cartoon critters, their big tails whipping and flourishing. They scampered across the grass, chattering at and razzing each other. O.T. was fond of squirrel stew, I knew. Bonnie made fried squirrel, scrambled eggs and biscuits as a power breakfast. I was getting hungry, if not for squirrel meat.

I mounted my bike and headed home to beat the rain. The motion of pedaling cramped and finally shrank my erection—I had suffered a two-hour-long, park revery hard-on, and it ached as if it had got banged in a door.

What if Jane and I got married in August? We could become the most prolific lovers in human history. Say, 700 great fucks per year until we hit age fifty. Then 350 a year for another two decades. Then semi-retirement—cut back to three fucks per week until, wattled and arthritic, we croaked at eighty. Maybe 30,000 fucks if we stayed healthy and didn't start getting on each other's nerves.

I made that my mantra. It would have to buoy me until August. Chant silently: 30,000...30,000...30,000.

LITTLE RED
RIDING HOOD

*O*n Friday afternoon Jane arrived wearing a red-and-white striped blouse, a short red skirt, beige nylons, red garters, and a red beret—and she was on foot. Carloads of slavering would-be molesters must be smoldering along the roadside in her wake, like the punk jalopies in *The Road Warrior*. Jane looked criminally sexy. I felt like a slob in my I.R.S. records T-shirt and raggedy cutoffs and big bare feet with dirty untrimmed toenails.

I was too overwrought to talk. Jane cupped my ass as we kissed. I groaned. I put my hands on her butt and squeezed gently. I felt her thighs above her stocking tops. Warmth and softness. Whatever deity had designed Jane deserved worship, tribute, tithing, volcano sacrifices, goat slitting—the whole nine yards.

I made piña coladas and we got mildly drunk. Not so bombed that our nerve endings were blunted, though. I went into my bedroom and turned the fan on to cool things off. We stayed on the couch and necked like teenagers for a half hour. Jane upended the blender and drained the last froth. I licked away her colada mustache. I picked her up and carried her to bed.

I unstrapped Jane's shoes and slipped them off. I unzipped her dress and she shifted her hips and lifted it free. I unbuttoned her blouse and removed it. Jane was smiling and blushing and nibbling her lip. I undid her bra and out popped her perfect little tits. The nipples were hard pink candies, irresistible. I kissed and licked them.

My heart was doing a drum solo. I undressed in five seconds flat, scattering my shabby threads on the floor. Jane wriggled out of her panties, which had a pink snowflake pattern. She slipped out her tampon—I watched in awe. She put it in her panties and dropped them on the floor.

Jane sat on the bed and I caressed her warm tan back with its pale bikini-line. I felt her waist as she unpeeled her stockings. She slid up onto the bed against me. I lightly spread my hands over her kneecaps and stroked down to her ankles and back up, stirring an electrical charge. My palms tingled. Jane was looking at me and smiling.

I kissed into her smile. I licked the inside of her mouth. Heat flashed across my face and swept down my shoulders and chest and groin. A flash fire of erotic anticipation. I kissed Jane's breasts and licked down her belly. I could hear her heart knocking.

I came licking back upward and as I kissed her lips she seized my dick. Gently, like a burglar jimmying a door, she coaxed the first strand of jism loose. She rubbed it on my thigh. I was above her, my hands shaping her breasts. I eased into her and we both gasped. I shut my eyes and stroked. The sweet sensation crested quickly. I paused at the apex and waited for Jane to climb up with me. I could feel her clutching and contracting. Her blunt fingernails dug in my back. I was too excited to hold myself any longer. I flooded Jane blissfully. I could feel it in my scalp, my feet, and everywhere in between—an emotional and physical gushing.

We lay together in the cool wash of the fan. Jane kissed my chest and teased my nipples, which were super sensitive. I stroked her hair, touched her cheek. No need to say a word. Love and sex were in a realm beyond spoken language. I could feel the stickiness below, our mingled juices and Jane's blood.

I could not stop myself from crying a little. Jane soothed me with kisses and didn't protest my tears. I knew that in her family emotional displays were not popular. My own family tradition was volatile and even hyper-emotional. I had seen my dad weep listening to music. I had to retire my copy of Mahler's *Third Symphony* because when I played it I remembered my dad crying, and it lacerated me. There were so many emotional sounds of my parents in my memory—I heard my dad vocalizing his passion and my mother crying out in response at the peak of their lovemaking during their habitual weekend afternoon "naps." My mom, too, was labile. Waltz music, a beautiful landscape, a helpless animal—so many things could set her off. Dewey had his bachelor stoicism and his low-key geniality, yet he wept to Hank Williams records or Neil Young's "Cortez the Killer." I was in this tradition. Unhappiness stunned me and made me silent and introspective, but happiness could tear loose my strongest emotion and make me cry.

Jane ran her fingers through my long messy curly hair and kept kissing me like an angel of comfort and mercy. She didn't mind the snot or the hot salty overspill of tears. Her toes brushed my calf.

"You're a train wreck, Bud," she said at last.

"I'm sorry."

"Don't apologize. I don't want Mr. Blasé for a lover. Where's the fun in that?"

"That's good." I pinched my wet eyelids.

"We should take a shower and then change these sheets. They're kinda Draculaed." She made a croaking laugh.

"Let me kiss your body for a while first."

"Stay above the waist, okay Jose?"

I made a snuffling laugh. "I'm not promising that." I kissed stepwise down her belly. I rested my chin on her hairy delta.

"Bud…"

I kept going. I tasted her rich, salty, bloody, tender slit. I lapped Jane, loving the taste, the forbidden thrill. Essence of life, blood and love-juice. I slid my head over her thigh and turned Jane into the spooning position and smooched her rump. I had always wanted to kiss and lick the intimate pink rosebud between her round cheeks, and now I did. Jane sighed deeply. She trembled. I licked her joyously, round and round her flexing, relaxing bud. A delicious musky fleshy taste. Instantly I was transformed into an analingus devotee.

When I came up for air, Jane's face was flushed with heat. Such a beautiful girl. I caressed her face and we both smiled.

"Well, you dog, you had the grand tour. Happy now?"

"Yep."

We took a shower together. I gargled like a hippo in a pond. I soaped Jane's bush and butt and washed her tenderly. She did the same for me. The soap suds stung the tip of my dick, but I didn't complain. Johnson's should market a no-sting dick soap. It'd be a big seller. We lathered each other's hair and rinsed in the warm waterfall, kissing and blowing water on each other.

"See how good you taste?"

Jane pinched my ass lightly. "Not too bad, considering."

"I'm not brushing my teeth tonight, I wanta savor it."

"Suit yourself."

We toweled each other dry and used the hair blower. Jane got a tampon from her purse and I watched her insert it.

"Damn, I wish I had some film in my camera."

I sprawled on my bed in my cutoffs and watched Jane dress languidly. "Let's listen to music and taper off here, Bud. I'm wrung out." She put her stockings and garters in her purse—a jumbo white thing the size of a baseball base. She wrapped the used tampon in Kleenex.

"We should put that one in Omar's pillowcase."

"That could touch off a war."

"Hell, he'd probably have it for a midnight snack."

"Bud!" Jane whacked me on the bicep.

She set the mussed tampon on my bed table next to my Flannery O'Connor book.

I carried Jane back to the living room—both as a symmetrical ceremonial gesture and because I wanted to. We drank iced tea and listened to Fairport Convention's *Unhalfbricking* and Robyn Hitchcock's *Groovy Decay*—the cream of the British musical empire, nonmainstream division. Jane was a good listener, though she could be maddeningly literal-minded at times.

Cleveland was not a hotbed for alternative rock or college rock or whatever the fuck you wanted to call it, and Jane was a victim of all the bad radio stations. When you've been discoed and Fleetwood Mac'd for years, Robyn Hitchcock can sound awfully bent.

When the first side of *Groovy Decay* was over, she nudged me hard. "That 52 Stations' song gave me the creeps. Is it a breakup song or a murder song? You can't tell."

"Whichever it is, it's a great song. It's *obsessive*. I think it's more the fantasy or threat of murder. You have to accept the strange and the ambiguous when you're listening to Robyn."

We did some snuggling until 4:45 and I got hopelessly excited again. "Five weeks!" I whined.

"Yes, but think how *gooood* it'll feel in August. We'll be like Diane Keaton and Warren Beatty in *Reds* when they were reunited."

"Warren was too pooped to screw at that point, if I remember. That movie's like novocaine except for Henry Miller. Old Warren should have just let Henry spiel for three hours."

"You lying shit, you told me you liked it when we saw it. Were you patronizing me? Afraid to antagonize your little dolly?"

"Simmer down. You know I love to antagonize you. I never said I liked it. I liked Diane Keaton. God, I love women when their faces turn pink and their eyes blaze. You and Diane..."

"*Reds* is a good movie. You better drive me home, shithead."

"Yes'm."

My car was steamy with garage-baked heat. Jane goosed me as I backed out. "Yeah, Diane in a stocking cap trekking across Norway. That *was* good."

"Just shut up about it. And it wasn't Norway."

I turned the radio on. We drove with the windows down and Steppenwolf's "Born to Be Wild" blasting, annoying everyone we passed.

"You understand this one okay?"

"Go shit in your hat."

"I see you smiling."

"Watch the road."

I pulled up in front of Jane's house. We kissed on the heated seat. I plunged my hands into her thick mane of honey-blond and sable-and-tan hair—autumn and earthen colors. I flopped across the seat, my feet wedged under the steering wheel, and put my head in Jane's lap and inhaled her scent.

"Well. See you in August," Jane said matter-of-factly. She tousled my hair and tweaked my ears. She smiled at me.

I got upright to face her. "I love you with all my heart, Jane."

"I know you do. I love you too, Bud." She squeezed my bare knee. A casual touch but it pierced me. Her fingers slid off as she opened the door. She slammed the door and strode up the walk to her front porch. She turned and grinned and I was walloped by emotion.

I didn't call out. I honked the horn and made a blind U-turn and drove home, numb and devastated. I would have to find something drastically distracting to get through the next five weeks.

Part
Two

MEG

$\mathcal{T}$he universal law of reversal sat on my chest like a load of bricks. Dewey spent the weekend getting reacquainted with Meg, who was back from Lexington, Kentucky. And Omar, against all odds, had mesmerized a fourteen-year-old Ramones acolyte named Trudy—braces, shaggy hornet's nest hairdo, flamingo legs. She looked like a sci-fi adolescent version of Shelley Duvall. If she mated with Omar, their children would be goofy mutants. But what the hell—anyone who could occupy Omar's time was a godsend.

Afternoons I hung out at Dewey's store, benefitting from the air-conditioning. A summer in Cleveland can be a preview of hell. The sidewalks were like griddles, the air thick with humidity.

Saturday night Zak and I went to the last surviving drive-in in Cuyahoga County and saw a double feature of *The Hunger* and *The Sender,* upscale horror movies that weren't too exhilarating.

Zak brought a cooler full of Stroh's, a decent working man's beer that helped blunt the dull movies. We perked up during the lesbian seduction scene in *The Hunger,* but it was too evasive to expose much. Exploitation moviemakers were losing their knack. Whenever I thought of Susan Sarandon, I flashed to the lemons in the crisper of our refrigerator. And remembered the creosote and sun-baked stone aromas of New Orleans, which we'd visited in the summer of '75. *Atlantic City* and *Pretty Baby*—much happier experiences than *The Hunger.*

Between movies I went to the concession stand and bought us cheeseburgers in silver-foil wrappers—gluey nuclear-waste cheese and formaldehyde-tasting pickles microwaved into the patty. *The Sender* had one good scene when the spooky telekinesis-sufferer overloaded and burst awake during a medical operation, spraying bodies and scalpels and trays all over the room. Zak had quaffed half a dozen Stroh's and was enjoying himself.

I got home at 1:30 and spent the night getting up to piss every two hours. At least wine flushed you out in one hellacious gusher. Beer worked its revenge a drizzle at a time.

I spent Sunday regretting what I'd agreed to the day before. Zak conned me into working on the night crew at Pellardi's. July was a big month for vacationing, and also some schmuck on the crew had injured himself. So there was an immediate opening. Zak phoned me at noon and confirmed my acceptance. I'd have some extra money to spend on Jane in August, and physical labor might curb my hyper sex drive. Or at least make me sleepy.

I listened to Marianne Faithfull records, drank a little vodka, and stayed in an empathetic funk until sundown. I was tempted to read *The Bell Jar,* which Jane had pressed on me, but kept enough sanity to nix that idea. I was grateful that Omar was spending the night at Kevin's.

At 9:30 Dewey and Meg arrived. Meg was pitching a bitch about the heavy German dinner they'd had, and Dewey put on Willie Nelson's *Red-Headed Stranger* album to mollify her.

"That damn gravy's denser than sewer mud. I'm gonna shit a wet cannonball pretty soon."

"This woman's a living diary of her bowel movements, Bud," Dewey said. He fixed Meg an Alka-Seltzer with a twist of lime and grabbed Rolling Rocks for himself and me.

Meg buttonholed me. "What ails you, Bud? You barely say hello. You sit there like a hound with a nut wound."

Meg was a svelte redhead—skinny legs and bit tits, a prototypical Kentucky–West Virginia hell-raising babe. "Hi Meg. Hi for the second time. You were too busy grousing to notice the first one. I'll get up and shred some ticker tape and toss it around if you insist." I grinned despite my bad mood. I liked Meg a lot.

Meg put a finger on my eyelid and peered at me. "You need a pump and a trim. If I didn't feel like a gorged python, I'd take you home and do you up, down and sideways. You know I'm a sucker for that hippie look of yours." She hefted a handful of my hair. "And Dewey'll be kerblooey by eleven."

Dewey chortled. "She's gonna hit me with a sap and molest my kid nephew. Won't work, Meg. Bud's avoiding robust women on principle."

"Shut up, everybody!" Meg commanded silence so that we could listen to Willie's classic shitkicker ballad, "Blue Eyes Crying in the Rain."

When the song was over, she continued: "So your little doll split for the summer. Big em-effin' deal. Get another one! Comb your hair, put on some decent clothes, and haul your buns over to the mall. Show some spirit. That mall's like a cathouse on free-sample day. Droves of teenage girls. Believe my words, Bud."

"Bud'd never cheat on Jane. Huh, Bud?" Dewey was uncharacteristically sadistic, egging me on to entertain Meg.

I shook my head in disgust. I acted the prig.

"Cheatin's in cards and income tax. Go get some pussy, give some girl a thrill. That's not cheatin'. That's life."

"Cool it, Meg. Act like a lady."

"You call me a 'lady,' I'll bite the 75 bottom out of your butt, Bud."

"How do you put up with this terrorism, Dew?" Everybody's belly was starting to tremble with silent mirth.

"Stay sedated and wear a cup over my balls."

"I gotta go shit *now*." Meg teetered off the couch.

"Turn the fan on in there."

I flipped the record and got us two more beers. The faint sound of Hawaiian percussion and Don Ho's voice emanated from Bob Steingruber's house. Bob was celebrating the Sabbath the only way he knew how.

"We should play that Nina Hagen record for Meg," I said. "In keeping with the theme of Teutonic torment."

"Don't even suggest it, Bud. Meg'd shit right on the couch."

Meg returned, fanning herself with an old copy of *Creem,* Omar's preferred constipation-time reading matter. Meg was not about to let a good crap go undescribed. "I hope that bomb passes through your pipes without rupturing 'em, Dewey. It was like the Dairy Queen machine gone haywire. Every piece had a squiggle on the end of it..."

"How 'bout a glass of water, Meg," I said. "You're so pale your freckles look like measles."

"Get me an American beer and be quick."

Dewey switched on the news at eleven. The top story was another sighting of the Nude Prowler. Some doofus was traipsing around the suburbs nocturnally—butt-naked, limp-hosed probably, and squawking at old ladies on their screened porches.

"Sounds like my first husband Harry's out on parole," Meg said.

Meg mellowed out enough to tolerate some garage rock. Dewey played two custom-made tapes back to back, and we all got drunk listening to the Nashville Teens, the Standells and ? and the Mysterians. I went to bed in a daze and I heard Meg and Dewey giggling like teenagers as they undressed each other and segued into a belly-sloshing screw.

THE CREW

*O*n the way to work Monday night Zak and I shared a bomber to take the edge off the loathsomeness of the hours ahead. I wasn't much of a dope smoker, having seen too many brain-damaged tokers in high school and legions more in college. But this was an emergency.

When we arrived at 8:50 I met Krupyak, the crew chief. He had a Captain Ahab stride—although both legs seemed made of flesh and bone—and every drink he'd ever slugged down showed in the maroon, violet and crimson headcheese of his schnozz. He shook my hand and packed some snuff in his jaw. He gave me a time card and a W-2 to fill out.

A couple bag-boys, teenage buffoons, were setting up the conveyer belt in the center aisle. Zak wheeled aside a bread rack and unlatched the shoulder-high door behind it. Warm air and diesel fumes gushed in. The delivery truck backed up to the opening and braked with a hot wheeze.

The driver was a trog—hulking, hirsute, with a big protuberant gut. He wore a blue bandanna on his head. "Hot fucker tonight! Whew! My balls are sweatin' like a wet sponge." He smiled broadly. He had twenty teeth in his head, tops. Could be a peanut-brittle abuser.

"We don't need no updates on your balls, Herbie," Krupyak said.

The rest of the crew straggled in. There were six poor devils in all. Tuts—a short, mushroom-pale, ageless drip in thick glasses. Muff—a tall, jittery lurp who had been a year ahead of Zak and me in school. The Gunner—another skinny, gangly guy, wearing goggles and a pink T-shirt with a faded cartoon orgy on the back. And Pickle Juice—bearded, grungy, a ringer for the hombre who gets shot into a mud puddle in old western movies. Zak made five and I made six.

Two hefty girls lingered in the cookie aisle, reading the ingredients on a package of Double Fudge Oreos. "Yoohoo, girls! Closin' time!" Krupyak bellowed. Ducking under the conveyer belt, the girls lumbered toward the checkout counter with their chocolate goodies. A chill came over me as I heard the faint tinkle of Muzak in the empty store. "These Boots Are Made for Walking" as interpreted by the Outer Space String Ensemble.

"Does this shit play all night?" I asked Zak.

"Nah. Pickle Juice hooks his boombox up to the P.A. system."

There were six aisles on each side of the belt. Zak took soup/vegetables and condiments/ salad dressing. I got trapped in canned fruit/juice and baking suppplies/ Jell-O. Cartons started to whiz down the sloped line. It took me an hour or so to get the hang of the abbreviations on the sides of the boxes.

Tuts manned the toilet paper/Kleenex/Kotex and the pet supplies aisles. He had a one-quarter smile on his face at all times and did everything with underwater slowness. When the big cartons of paper towels began to bump together and back up, I edged over to help him.

Pickle Juice limboed under the conveyer belt and pitched in, too, booting Tuts in the ass as he passed him. "Tell Bud here your secret, Tuttle," he said.

Tuts grinned vacantly.

"Wait till break time," Pickle Juice said.

We unloaded over 1200 cartons by midnight. I hadn't realized how pampered and out of shape I was. I was winded and sweaty. The difference between fucking Jane and hauling cartons was dramatic—a chasm.

Krupyak and Herb the driver played two-handed poker in the back room, and the crew sat on boxes in the cereal aisle for a break party. Pickle Juice tugged two four-packs of wine coolers out of the cold case and everybody except Tuts and the Gunner snatched two bottles apiece.

"Not as good as beer, but it fucks the bastards out of more money," Zak said.

The Gunner had a quart of grape juice and an eight-dollar container of macadamia nuts. Tuts had some string cheese and a can of warm pop. Muff had baloney and a jar of Poupon mustard. Pickle Juice was the most ingenious—he had set two packages of frozen Swedish meatballs in a pan full of water on the huge electric light fixture, and it had slowly boiled up as we unloaded. I was too disgusted and tired to eat anything. Three hours of slob-labor had reduced me to a victim in an Upton Sinclair novel. *What a baby,* I said to myself. Jane's right.

"Fess up, Tuttle," Pickle Juice said. "Tell Bud your love-god secret...How many women have you ravished in a ravishing capacity?"

"'Bout thirteen."

"He can't be sure...Okay, whatta these unfortunate slits all have in common?"

"They were drunk."

"We assume that, micro-brain. What else?"

"All outweighed me."

Muff made a jungle caw. "Thirteen drunken grungolas and every one of 'em porky enough to judo-kick this gerbil across the parking lot. What are the Las Vegas odds on such a sexual history?"

"Seven thousand to one," Tuts said. He scratched his nose and gnawed a cheese whip.

"Those oddsmakers never hung out at the West Side Polkateria or they'd adjust it to seven to one. That place is crawling with hogs."

Zak had mentioned the sexual peccadilloes of the Gunner (hair-trigger ejaculator, known to ruin pants in public), Pickle Juice (kept his jizz in a pickle jar, funneled it into balloons on April Fools' Day, and balloon-bombed the quad at Western Reserve University), and Muff (excessively preoccupied with oral sex, which he'd never had in reality). I wondered if blue-collar labor led to erotic moronism. Tony was a ten-fingered assault demon and Zak, perpetually girlfriendless, liked to tell jokes with punchlines like "I said *sit* on my face, not *shit* on my face."

The crew did have renaissance   79   tendencies. Besides Tuts's polka-hall

Casanova record they discussed stock-car racing, handguns, the nutritional value of Sugar Pops, and *Return of the Jedi.* I had never considered Princess Leia an object of lust, but the Gunner pined for her. As an outsider and tyro, I kept quiet.

Just before the end of the break, Muff challenged me. "Hey Bud, you ever suck titties in a moving vehicle?"

"Maybe. What of it?"

"That's why you got hired."

"I got hired to suck titties? Why didn't somebody explain it to me? How come I had to lug all those fuckin' boxes instead?"

"Nah. Ray Worley, the guy you're replacing, he's a one-eyed motherfucker as of last Wednesday. He was suckin' his girlfriend's tits on the backseat of the car, like his brother was drivin'...Car went over the railroad tracks and—yick...Got his eye poked out by a tit nipple."

"It was just an abrasion," Pickle Juice said.

"Puncture."

"He'll be back."

"Okay. Let me ask you this then, Bud. Ever eat pussy with your eyes open?"

"I took a peek once or twice."

"Not wise. Another good way to lose an eye."

"I'll consider welder's goggles in the future."

This concluded the optical safety tips, as Krupyak gimped out of the back room and clanged the metal conveyer belt with a slat. "Back to work, you fuckers! And dispose of those goddamn wine bottles, or it's my ass!"

As the two crew members with the lowliest status, Tuts and I had to break down the conveyer line by sections and push the rickety cart that housed it into the back hallway next to the garbage compactor, which reeked of rotten produce. A rat scurried in front of us and Tuts ground to a stop, jamming the cart into my shins. This place was a hellhole.

All night long we fetched and lifted like zombies. My body ached as if I'd been beaten with a sockful of gravel. The only thing that kept us semi-alert was the heavy metal bombardment from the boombox. I finally understood the utility of Motorhead and Black Sabbath and the Scorpions: artificial adrenaline for night crews.

I drank bottled water and munched Tums—the wine coolers had stirred heartburn. From four A.M. to six A.M. we pulled all the merchandise forward, straightening the shelves to entice tomorrow's glassy-eyed shoppers. I pictured purblind nipple-puncture victims groping for canned okra.

From six A.M. to seven A.M. we stocked the dairy case, which smelled like a buttermilk belch. Krupyak gave us ratshit details like rotating the cheese and yogurt by the stamped expiration dates. To ream the store out of a little profit, Zak crammed the soon-to-decay product behind the fresh stuff. In fact, everybody adopted this system. None of us was a primo candidate for a missile silo job.

At 7:15 Krupyak hobbled up and down the aisles, inspecting our handiwork. He liberated us. "I'll see you pickle-dicks tomorrow."

"Some fun, huh?" Zak said. The parking lot was foggy and barren. The air was already muggy. I felt nine-tenths comatose. The Gunner climbed into his bashed-in jalopy next to us. Tuts squeegeed the windshield of his pea soup–colored Ford. Pickle Juice and Muff carpooled in a van, rubbed down to gray primer—a serial killermobile.

Zak dropped me off and I went inside quietly. Before taking a shower, I wrote Dewey a note and put it under his car keys. DEWEY—TELL OMAR *ABSOLUTELY* TO KEEP QUIET UNTIL 4 P.M. I'LL MASSACRE HIM IF HE WAKES ME UP. THANKS—BUD.

Damp and sore—and mercifully limp-noodled—I went to sleep.

THE

CONTESTANT

I woke up at 4:30 in the afternoon, sweaty and disoriented and depressed. I had to go to work in a little over four hours. It was July 3rd, and tomorrow was our annual celebration—beer blast, extended picnic, and firecracker skirmish.

I took a cool shower to wake myself up. As I dried myself, I heard loud banging. Wrapped in a towel, I walked into the living room. Omar was hanging a bird cage on the wall, the bird sloshing back and forth on its perch and squawking. There was plaster dust on the floor and a jar full of nails and screws. He hammered away savagely.

Trudy gave me a toothy grin. "Hi Bud."

"Don't flash my girlfriend, honky," Omar said.

"Hi Trudy. Omar, you'd look cute with a claw-hammer up your ass."

"Pretty vacant," the parakeet said, steady on its perch.

I retreated to my room and put on my cutoffs. I was powerfully hungry. I'd have to brave Omar's belligerence to use the kitchen.

"What's the bird's name?" I asked Trudy. From its perch it tilted its ass and crapped a sour-cream dollop onto the floor of the cage. I couldn't fathom the attraction of a caged bird.

"Sid."

I made two salami-and-lettuce-and-tomato sandwiches and drank about a quart of water to stave off dehydration and heartburn. On the table was a yellow paper flyer.

ATTENTION ASSHOLESFIFTH ANNUAL 4TH OF JULY FARTING CONTEST***$3 ENTRY FEE***SAM THE BLAM SIMPKINS—OFFICIAL JUDGE***4 P.M. SHARP BRAINARD FIELD BY THE BACKSTOP***RULES AND ENTRY FORM ATTACHED***

I saw the staple mark where Omar had ripped the second page off. "You gonna enter this thing, ass-blast? At last a sport that you can excel at."

"I'm gonna win."

Trudy grimaced. "He's in training. Pretty gross."

"Six bran muffins, onion soup, a macaroni dinner and some microwave popcorn for the Gatling-gun effect...That was lunch. Trudy's gonna make me burritos for dinner."

"Trudy, you're gonna develop a warped psyche hangin' out with this nuclear-gas reactor."

"Too late to stop, we're stuck in the slop, your uncle's a Wop," Omar crooned. He whirled and cut a soft fart in my direction.

I splashed cold water on my face. "Omar—plug your ass or leave. Show a little consideration for Trudy at least."

Backed up against the stove, I started to eat a peach.

"She—loves—me—just—the—way—I—am...That's a Billy Jowls tune for all you bozos out in bozoland. Let's motor, babe." He took Trudy by the elbow and she giggled. "Don't eat my bird while I'm gone, salami-breath."

I was still feeling melancholy, so I put on Jackson Browne's *Late for the Sky* album. With its dead girlfriends and dope-addled ruminations, it was a nifty downer. To counteract it I played the Neville Brothers' *Fiyo on the Bayou* and then some Chuck Berry, which always energized me.

Dewey arrived at 8:30 carrying a pizza. "What the hell's with the bird? Aunt Tess been here?"

"Naah. Trudy and Omar are starting a menagerie."

"Where is the little punk?"

"Enchanting Trudy and her family with his talking asshole."

He shook his head. "Hope they're not of the P.T.A. or P.T.L. persuasion. How'd the job go?"

"Oh I'm a real craftsman now. I think I'll join the guild."

"Horrible, huh?"

"The only good thing was when some klutz dropped a carton of spaghetti sauce. That shit makes a terrific gory mess."

"Tough it out for a month. It'll help you appreciate the record store."

"Don't worry. I already appreciate it."

"Here's a card from Jane." He sifted through the mail, which was piled on the greasy pizza carton, and handed me a postcard.

A picture of a jetty, a lighthouse, the dark blue Atlantic. I flipped it over. "Dear Bud, Freddie set a new world's record for obnoxiousness on the drive from Ohio. Dad threatened to cut his tongue out and sell him to cod fishermen. I'm reading *Wise Blood*—much better and meaner than magnolia-blossom Southern fiction. Visit Mandingo at the kennel on Mayfield if you get lonesome for the Simmons touch. The salt ocean air reminds me of our bedsheets during good times. Wish you and B.B. were here so I could have the real thing. Love, Jane."

B.B. stood for Big Boy, Jane's affectionate nickname for my dick, which was average size but starting to flex as I reread the message. I sniffed the card, hoping for an emanation from Jane, but I couldn't detect any.

Zak would be here in fifteen minutes. I got my work clothes on, and Dewey gave me two slices of pizza and a beer for fortification. He set the Chuck Berry record back on side one. I wished I was breezing through the southland in a convertible, the radio blasting and Jane pressed against me.

"What's this Old Milwaukee piss?" I said. "Rolling Rock go toes up?"

"It was on sale."

"They should give it away." I guzzled the last of the mediocre beer as Zak pulled in. "S'long, Dew."

"Keep your spirits up, Bud. Tomorrow we party. And it could be worse—you could be in the army."

"I hear ya."

Zak was high on cough syrup. "Gotta switch around to avoid addictive behavior," he explained. We peeled out and I waved to Bob Steingruber, who was massacring the roadside weeds with a weed-cutter. Bonnie saluted from the lawn chair on her front porch. She was wearing white shorts and a white T-shirt over her jumbo bra. A fertility goddess at twilight.

Work was less tortuous than the first night. We unloaded a mere 700 cartons. Zak and I cleaned the meat cases while the other four studs humped the goods onto the shelves. I felt like a proctologist examining the big cats at the Cleveland Zoo—putrid odors lurked in the cases. We hosed down the meat trays and wiped them dry and diapered them with thick plastic pads.

Nobody was completely tuckered at break time, so we amused ourselves by pitching biscuit dough at the tile ceiling, which was already barnacled with dry dabs from past revels. I drank a quart of milk to outfox my incipient pizza-salami heartburn.

"What's the deal on this Nastassia Kinski broad?" Muff asked, a crooked grin on his urchin mug.

"Great-looking woman," I said.

"You see the one where that batshit ballet dancer played the fiddle on her. Jeez…"

"I missed that one. I saw *Cat People* and that junkyard one that Francis Ford Whatchamacallit made."

"Imagine yodeling Nastassia. Jeez…She'd be moanin' in some cockamamy foreign language…What is she, Polish?"

"What's it matter?"

"You'll never find out," Pickle Juice said. "Nastassia won't return your phone calls."

"I'll find her. We'll get us a big round bed, satin sheets, eat us some oysters," Muff said deliriously. "Bruce Lee tongue action. Heeeww. Hoooww. Haaahh."

"You're ravin'," the Gunner said. "No oysters, no Nastassia."

Krupyak rapped the stanchion. "Work time, fuckers."

We finished our stocking and rearranging and ritual sabotage by six A.M., and Krupyak dismissed us with an abusive snarl. "Looks like shit, but what am I gonna do. Jerry Lewis should hold a telethon for this bunch. Have a happy fourth a July, you twiddle-dicks."

"Fuck you, too, Krupe," Pickle Juice hollered. Krupyak's gargoyle face twisted into a grin. He waved from the door.

I didn't feel too bad. I needed a short snooze before the festivities started at noon.

CHOPPING TIME

*T*he kitchen smelled like a cross between a juice bar and a compost heap. Dewey was up to his elbows in watermelon meat, discarding the slippery black seeds and gouged-out rinds in a colander, dropping the seedless pieces in a punch bowl. Omar butchered honeydews and muskmelons, cramming wads of seeds and pulp into the colander.

"Go pour this out, dogboy," he said.

"There's coffee made," Dewey said. "Get enough sleep?"

"Yeah." I slugged down a mug of coffee, then walked out to the edge of the field and emptied the sloshing colander on the mulch pile.

Wearing low-fitting jeans that exposed the crack of his ass and a shrunken T-shirt that exposed his inner tube of bellyfat, O.T. was on all fours, painting the big rock near his backdoor white. He had a quart of beer in his left hand.

"Hey O.T., is the whole clan gonna be here?" I called.

"Ever'body but Daddy. If the resurrection hits, he'll be here too. I bet that mammyjammer's thirsty by now."

Thirsty ghouls—sounded like one of Omar's songs. "Tell Bonnie I'll be over to help her in a little bit."

"Okey doke."

Back in the kitchen, Omar was blending a Kaopectate-and-carob milk shake. He had two cream-cheese sandwiches on the counter.

I poured more coffee. "What happens if you shit your pants during a match?"

"Disgraced and disqualified."

"I'd be worried. You look bloated."

"Not everybody's a squish-ass like you."

"We're not in the society register," Dewey said. "A little flyin' shit won't ruin our good name."

Just to irritate Omar, I put the Ives *Second Symphony* on the stereo. Omar wasn't enough of a visionary to see Charles Ives as the precursor of Iggy Pop, Joey Ramone and Johnny Thunders. He made some peeved-gorilla facial expressions, but said nothing.

I scanned the morning paper, which had a fife-and-drum motif around the border and the usual horseshit holiday stories—ninety-two-year-old marathon bike riders, barbershop quartet showdowns, three-legged Seeing Eye dogs. Reagan looked like Howdy Dowdy in a cowboy hat. No news on the Nude Prowler.

"Chop chop, dump the slop," Omar said.

I humored him. I wasn't in the mood for conflict. I was in the mood to kiss every square inch of Jane's body. I took the colander out back and jettisoned it—there was a bug jamboree going on in the previous spillage. I heard a scuffle next door. O.T.'s girlfriend Jewel, a blocky wide-shouldered blonde in a I ♥ TO DO NUTHIN sweatshirt, was drinking O.T.'s beer, and he was flicking paint at her ankles.

"Come over here and gimme a hug, Bud."

"Just a second, hon'."

I took the colander in and went out the front door and across the burgeoning crabgrass patch of our side lawn. Jewel had knocked O.T. on his side and painted his neck partially white. She used my legs to hoist herself.

"Watch out, Bud. She's in attack mode."

I smelled mayonnaise and onions on Jewel as she embraced me. She was a big woman. She could have kept Tuts's streak going easy.

"Damn if you don't look like a subversive with that mess of hair." She rubbed her nose against my cheek and grabbed two handfuls of hair. She kissed me on the mouth to tease O.T., who didn't seem to mind. She definitely had me outmuscled. Jewel worked as a dog shampooer, and the fruity dog soap scent clung to her sweatshirt along with the potato-salad effluvia. I bet she was a wild and jolly lay. She sure kept O.T. happy.

"When's this lazy hunk of butt-cake gonna marry you, Jewel?"

Jewel snorted. "When's he gonna get his blubberboy body upright?"

O.T. painted her toes from a kneeling position. "Never. We's strictly an open-love team."

"Yeah, Liz Taylor might come back on the market and he has to keep his options open." Jewel rubbed her wet toes on O.T.'s shirt.

"I'll let you and Liz face off in a fried-chicken scarfin' contest, Jewel. The winner gets me."

"Let's go inside, Bud. Let Leonardo here work in isolation." Jewel snatched the quart of beer from the grass.

There were sleeping bags on the living room floor and a stack of O.T.'s favorite videos next to Bonnie's VCR—*Ms. 45, Prophecy, The Funhouse.*

Rayford was in the kitchen, dicing onions in the maniacal style of an Oriental chef. Bonnie was crying from the fumes.

"Hi Bud. Ten onions and I'm a wreck."

Cold chopped potatoes filled a tub the size of a junior coffin. Bonnie wiped her eyes and dumped a bowl of red bell pepper shards into the white mound.

Then black olives and diced pickle and spices galore and gobs of horseradish mustard, which triggered more tears.

Jewel pinched my bare nipple.

"Mind your manners, Jewel. Bud's touchy."

"Abuse 'em and lose 'em—that's my new motto."

"Comin' through." Rayford upended the cutting board and spilled onions into the mix. He had wet nuggets in each nostril and on the edge of his mustache. "Gimme a snotwipe, Ma."

Bonnie sopped up his leakage. The Burdette family's potato salad teamwork was admirable. Bonnie added more mayonnaise and stirred the salad with a big wooden spoon.

"What can I do?" I asked.

"You can shell the eggs with Jewel, honey. I'm making fifty deviled eggs."

Rayford sat on a stool and drank a beer as Jewel and I cracked the eggs. Bonnie halved them and mashed the hard yolks deftly.

"Where's brother Billy?" I asked.

"Buying ice."

Bonnie's three sons were all in their mid to late twenties, and all worked in construction. I think Rayford was the oldest and Billy the youngest, but it was hard to tell with this brood. Their daddy died the same year as my dad Roy, 1979. A lot of rust-belt patriarchs succumbed to an early death, a fact that made unemployment more and more attractive to me. Stymie mortality via shiftlessness.

O.T. barged in to get a supplementary beer, and Tony was trailing him. "Found me a thirsty straggler."

I broke my no-beer-before-breakfast mandate and joined Tony and O.T. in an Independence Day salute. Hell, it was an incendiary holiday. It would be fun to get beered up and rout some present-day Brits. Maybe a blunderbuss ambush on Kajagoogoo and Spandau Ballet and Duran Duran.

"Omar's goin' for the butthole of the year trophy at four," I announced. "Attendance is mandatory."

"Are those stinkards up to that nonsense again?" Bonnie said. "They had the cops after them last year."

"You should've entered, O.T.," Jewel said.

"Ah, I'm too damn old. They got a age cutoff.'"

"Let's go see what Bob's cookin' up," I said.

"Bob's not too creative," Bonnie said. "I bet it's cherry Jell-O with fruit cocktail."

Bob's lawn was low and brown. He always set the blade on his lawn mower at scorched-earth level. I knocked on his rattletrap screen door and marched inside with Tony and O.T.

"Hey Bob, the neighborhood gourmet vigilantes wish to ascertain the nature of your contribution to the fiesta."

We filed into the kitchen, which was small and smelled like steamed cherries.

"Jell-O's my specialty. Can't fuck it up and it don't spoil."

"It's immortal, like." O.T. nudged Bob's foot. "What was never alive can't die."

Bob had his feet propped up on the table and he was reading a Grove Press perennial, *A Man with a Maid.*

"Did I lend you that, Bob?"

"Hell no. This is my own personal copy."

"Omar musta swiped mine then."

Bob broke out four cans of Miller.

"I'd ask you lugs to siddown if I had enough chairs."

"We hate to drink and run but we will," O.T. said.

We chugged our beers and flipped our empties into a trash bucket. I was apt to drink twenty beers before nightfall if I didn't pace myself.

"I'll be over to help set up the tables," Bob said.

"Wudga put in the Jell-O?" Tony said.

"Little pickled seahorses."

"You dog-fucker, I saw those empty fruit-cocktail cans."

"Why'd ya ask then?"

We split. As we walked across the street, Sam came out of the woods behind our house and trotted up to us. He was full of burrs and reeked of carrion.

"Good job, Sam," O.T. said. "You smell like the inside of a dead elephant's asshole. I'm gonna have to get old Jewel to freshen you up. The professional touch."

"She's bound to enjoy that," I said.

Tony and I went inside to check the melon-whacking progress. Dewey was digging out pale-green melon balls with a special scoop. Omar was flopped on the couch, kneading his stomach.

"Hi fartbag," Tony said.

"Pregame jitters," Dewey said.

"Fuck off."

I heard a car pull in. It was Charles and his girlfriend Lydia. They climbed out of his ancient VW, which was like a miniature bathysphere on wheels.

LYDIA AND
DANTON

$\mathcal{C}$harles was both keyed-up and sheepish as he introduced Lydia, who had so much makeup on that the excess might be satirical. She smiled ambiguously. Might mean, What is this shit? or Isn't this amusing, all these people floored by my tits? Her bosom *was* sensational. It knocked Tony gaga and set off sympathetic vibrations in my lips and fingertips.

Lydia wore a black snakeskin or some-kind-of-skin semi-transparent top and tight white shorts and big black open-toed clogs. Like Jane she painted her toenails red—a siren song to toe-suckers. Charles was wearing one of his science fair spaz outfits—an olive-and-beige short-sleeved striped shirt, baggy olive trousers, and black tennis shoes. He had the most hackneyed spaz accoutrement—masking tape around the sidepiece of his glasses where they'd popped a screw.

Dewey came outside and was the first one bold enough to run a line past Lydia— "Lydia! Try to rub some style off on Charles. I think he scares the New Wavers at the shop sometimes."

"Dock my pay," Charles cracked. "Hire some New Wave foofoo in a ruffled shirt and toreador pants."

"Oh, Charles is approaching perfection from a different angle," Lydia said. "You should let him work in a loincloth." She held Charles with one arm at the waist. Tony was hypnotized by Lydia's titties in their licorice-colored container, shimmying as she arched to buss Charles on his blushing cheek. Gimme one of those wet ones, I thought. I snapped my fingers in front of Tony's face.

Billy's truck came up the road, hauling a honeywagon on a pony cart. He backed up the Burdette driveway and swerved onto the side lawn. He clambered out of the cab—a shirtless, bearded 230-pound troll with rolls of rippling tan flab.

"Looky what I promoted, you all. Keep us from runnin' up our water bills, flushin' down that beer piss all day." We all walked over to check out the honeywagon, undoubtedly nabbed from a construction site. Billy unhitched the wagon and Tony and I helped him maneuver the little outhouse down the incline and set it on the grass.

"Interduce this beauty, you dummies," Billy said.

"Billy Burdette, meet Lydia. I think you know Charles."

"Sure. Bought me some tapes from Charlie a few weeks back. How'd you snag such a great-lookin' gal, Charlie?"

"Good fortune, Bill."

"Where's this legendary punk kid hiding?" Lydia asked.

Dewey chuckled. "Inside takin' a dump. Hope he doesn't eliminate his competitive edge."

"He's signed up for the annual farting contest," I said.

"Sounds like a blast. Can we go, Charles?"

Charles colored slightly and spread his hands. "And miss the chamber music concert and the quilting bee?"

Billy began to unload sacks of ice from the cab of his truck. Sam, freshly scrubbed, trotted over and examined the dike of ice sacks.

"You squirt on my ice, I'll kill ya, Sam."

A candy-apple red convertible with a raccoon tail on the aerial drove up the road and pulled into our driveway beside Charles's VW. It was Penny and her mystery suitor, who was tall and wore sunglasses and a Cubs baseball hat.

The motley crowd, except for Billy, shifted back to our yard. Omar came outside, squinting and cinching his belt, to greet Penny.

"Omar," Penny said. "Ready to bomb 'em dead?"

"I am...the Gasman." He waggled his butt.

Danton waved genially to the 93 crowd. Penny and Lydia hugged,

Lydia's knockers mooshing into Penny at shoulder level. Penny might've been the one who introduced Lydia to Charles. She had a broad range of friends and cronies—political activists, exotic dancers, local music-scene fringers, ex–high school hellcat types who lived in mobile homes out in Amish country. I wondered if Lydia was a bump-and-grinder.

We put tablecloths on the three picnic tables in our backyard. The maple trees gave us some cool shade. Danton had a cooler full of knockwurst, which he set against a tree trunk.

Lydia and Charles sat on a blanket holding hands. She whispered something in his ear which made him grin like a fiend. She might've offered to buff his head with her breasts later.

Penny explained Danton's current situation. "Danton's going to be a stand-up comedian, and not some David Brenner jerk, either. You watch. If we can get a few drinks in him, he might perform later." Danton was impassive, fiddling with his shades, stroking Penny's shoulder. "Trouble is, he just got fired from his job as a pizza chef. Tell them what happened, baby."

"Ah—same old excrement ball. Couple buddies rolled in Tuesday night with some magic mushrooms to have on their pizza. We got in a bit of rush and I lost track of the oven placement, kind of. Had three different mushroom and double cheeses going at once. Upshot of it is, the deluxe one got served to this family and they all went blotto and started seeing the mystical mastodon herds or whatever. My buddies were pretty pissed off and so was the manager. Spoiled their evening when they started munching and the wallpaper stayed the same color. Spoiled his evening when he had to be a paramedic with this family of straights. I could be facing a triple lawsuit... It was more like I resigned than actually got fired. Old Dave wouldn't fire a cook during the dinner rush if he found him baking body parts. He's not a bad guy, as managerial assholes go... I needed a change anyway. Trouble is, I got locked out of my apartment the same goddamn night—the old landlord-

94

slaps-on-a-padlock deal. Penny's saving my tail for the moment. Anybody bad-mouthing this woman will have to answer to me. I'm optimistic. I got a car, I got clean underwear, I got Penny. There may be an opening at Cho's Luau Heaven next week. I've cooked that Hawaiian slop before, I can do it again."

Dewey trundled out the back door with a washtub full of iced Rolling Rock. He set it next to the wurst-hamper. O.T. and Billy waded across the back lot, bearing portable BBQers. They looked like heralds in a Shakespeare in the Holler production, their bellies jiggling, both cursing and kicking at Sam, who capered along beside them.

"Put a big rock on that cooler or Sam'll have those wursts," Dewey said. I got a twenty-pounder from the border of a fern bed and weighted the cooler down.

Everybody but Charles had a beer. He claimed a queasy stomach. I heard dragging noises along our driveway. Bob wheeled a TV cart around the side of the house, with a turkey roaster full of Jell-O on the cloth trampoline straps and another plastic tub of Jell-O on top of the roaster. Bob wore powder-blue Bermuda shorts. He groaned as the jittery cart banged his hairless shins.

"Bob, you look like you're wearin' a hair shirt and a crown of thorns," Dewey said. "Here." He guided the cart into the shade and gave Bob a beer.

"We need ice," I said. "Or Bob's Jell-O masterpiece'll go sour on us."

"I'm takin' shit for my Jell-O again."

"Sip that beer and relax, Bob," Dewey said. "Massage Bob's shins, Lydia, before they turn purple."

Lydia slid over and rubbed Bob's shins. I watched for the up periscope effect in Bob's Bermudas. I had to help O.T. with the ice detail, though. We moseyed over to their garage and filled two tubs of ice. I ducked into the kitchen—Bonnie and Jewel were bombarding plates of deviled eggs with paprika.

We hoisted our tubs and ferried them over and cooled down Bob's Jell-O. Omar dozed under the tree next to Penny and Danton, and Sam slept next to him with his head on his paws.

95

Dewey brought two speakers outside onto the patio, which was overgrown with crabgrass and dandelions. He put some Otis Redding on the stereo. Omar came awake and protested. "I hate this Memphis soul shit."

"Many of the greats are from Memphis," I razzed him. "Otis, Alex Chilton, Al Green…"

Another car pulled into our driveway. Zak shambled around the side of the house, carrying a cooler full of beer in his mitts and two bags of Doritos in his teeth.

"Look at this fucking circus act," Omar said.

Zak ejected the Doritos and lay the cooler in the shade. "Greetings, beer-lovers." I introduced Lydia and Danton. Zak sat down next to me and Tony and popped a beer and gawked at Lydia's chest. Omar broke open the Nacho-flavored Doritos and crunched a handful, adding to the cheese-and-sodium lava already massed in his gut.

"How's your ass, champ?" Zak said.

"Ready to meet your face."

Soothed by Lydia's fingers, Bob went on the attack. "Omar, people are gonna look at you and they're gonna decide t'stop havin' kids."

"See if I care. How come you didn't have any brats, Bob? Get your peenie tied in knots?"

"Omar," Dewey said.

"Mellow out, Omar," Penny said. She tickled his armpit.

"I'm stuck here with the Mellow Yellow crowd." He stuffed another handful of Doritos in his yap.

Bonnie yelled to O.T. and Billy, and they helped her and Jewel carry two card tables and the gigundo bin of potato salad across to our yard.

I fired up the two grills. We would indulge in round one of eating to keep the beer in our bellies company, then attend the big sphincter showdown en masse.

CHOW TIME

In the next twenty minutes the rest of the celebrants arrived—Meg, toting hamburger patties and buns; Trudy, carrying a pot of baked beans; Rayford, safariing trays of eggs across the back lot; and Kevin, bearing nothing but his appetite.

I let Billy and O.T. tend the grills so that I could stay even with Tony and Zak in the beer-drinking sweepstakes. We all felt a touch of self-pity at our womanless state. Tony's putative girlfriend Patty had disowned him for physical and spiritual misdemeanors—misuse of thumb during digital loveplay and failure to appreciate Rickie Lee Jones as a chanteuse.

"That groggy beatnik bimbo irritates me," Tony said. "Why try to hide it?"

"You might've slipped by on the Rickie Lee thing," I said. "But it's uncouth to slide your thumb up a girl's heinie."

Zak guffawed. "Not until the fourth or fifth date at least."

"Patty's a 4-H and a Rainbow Girl, Tony. They got these strict guidelines. You can't hold hands till you're engaged, practically."

"She let me take her panties off. Besides, it was a joke."

"Hey, we appreciate that. But trust me—that thumb-goosing thing *will never work*. Case closed."

Having skipped breakfast, and on my fifth or sixth beer, I was getting drunk. I needed some grilled meat.

Sam was alert and drooling at the smell of burgers. The Burdette brothers milled around the grills, poking each other and cussing. Bonnie helped to fix Trudy's braids—she'd scuttled her misshapen beehive—while Omar belittled her efforts.

"Okay if I wallop Omar one, Dewey?" Bonnie asked.

"Sure."

Omar fell on the lawn and performed a Three Stooges circular fit as Bonnie whacked him.

When the first batch of burgers was cooked, I snatched two and slapped on some mustard and relish. I hated ketchup, which made me a pariah condiment-wise. I spooned out a mound of potato salad and took my sagging plate and sat down at the base of the tree and dug in.

"Where's mine?" Meg said. "You got the manners of a jababby."

"I wasn't raised well."

"Blame your poor folks. That's right. It's a good thing you're cute, Bud. An ugly kid would get slapped silly for the shit you pull."

"That's a heartless analysis of human behavior, Meg. I know plenty of plug-uglies who get away with murder. Omar, for instance."

"Omar's growing into his body. And he could use a sympathetic barber. That's all...But in my experience the ugly definitely take more abuse."

Tony and Zak sat down next to me with their burgers and plate-soaking beans slipsliding into their potato salad.

"These plates leak."

"Sit at a table and they won't leak," Meg said.

"Use two plates for extra soppin' strength, you dumbshits," Billy said.

Omar tossed a gherkin in the air and caught it in his mouth. Sam licked his nose in excitement. Flying food was one of his turn-ons. Omar threw him a gherkin and he caught it like a gator.

"Let's go bug Meg," I said.

Zak and Tony and I bellied up to Meg's table and sat down. Trudy fed Omar beans by the spoonful. He shut his eyes and ate, savoring the taste and presentation.

I loaded up a spoon with chopped jalapeños and passed it to Trudy. She shook her head, grinning. "He'd kill us," she said. Omar opened one eye.

"Don't fuck around, you goombahs."

"Go back to sleep, beano," I said.

"Hey Meg," Zak said. "Any bus-driving jobs open for this year?"

"No, but I hear they're hiring at the zoo...Looking for elephant dildoes. Your head's just about the right size, Zak."

"How'm I gonna fight this hillbilly quota system? My life's ambition is t'drive one of those big orange buses."

"Try the zoo. There's something about the shape of your head that just says, 'Ram me.' "

Zak gave up. Meg was tough to beat in a shit-fling.

Billy started dealing out grilled knockwursts. Penny and Danton and Lydia and Charles had formed a clique with Bob Steingruber at the next table. Slight as she was, Penny could pack in the chow. She and Danton were feeding each other deviled eggs. Lydia winked a kohl-smeared eyelid toward our table. Charles fed her an olive. Slurp.

"Looks like a food orgy over there," Zak said. "Does that Lydia make your balls ache or what?"

"What'd Charles do?" Tony said. "Answer an ad and get lucky?"

"Hey Charles," Meg hooted. "These slobs are lusting after your sweetheart."

"Give us a break, Meg," I said. "We're horny and drunk and lonely."

"Never mind! They apologize."

"Suffer, you lame-os," Charles said. "Maybe Lydia'll let you dance with her later if you show the proper obeisance."

"Now we've been cast into outer darkness with all the other jackoffs," I said. "Thanks a bunch, Meg."

Meg laughed it off.

Omar was drinking cream soda through a straw. Trudy packed a towel around his neck and patted his back. He grunted and burped.

"I'll bet five bucks you crap your pants in the heat of competition," Tony said.

"You're on, ketchup-lips."

Tony wiped his mouth.

A little less woozy with some food in me, I got another round of beers for our forlorn threesome.

"Where's mine?" Meg bitched.

"Here ya go, dragon lady." I gave her mine and went back to the washtub for another. Dewey sat down with two knockwursts swimming in beans.

"Is this mob getting on your nerves, Meg?"

"I could use a hit of Wild Turkey."

"Go get the Wild Turkey, Bud."

Inside I turned over the Otis Redding record and grabbed the bottle from the liquor cabinet. A trick rubber spider with a card Scotch-taped to it descended from the cabinet latch. STAY OUT OF THE BOOZE, OMAR. SIX WEEKS GROUNDED IF YOU DISOBEY—DEWEY. I was tempted to bring the tequila along, but decided to wait until sundown to kick off the real debauch.

Damn, I missed Jane. I could taste her lips. I could smell her skin and hair, as vivid and particular as warm bread pudding or new-mown grass. I had a hot flash of myself inside her, and the bottle of Wild Turkey slipped from my fingers and hit the rug with a thump. Lucky for me, it didn't bust.

When I got back to the party, I relieved Billy and O.T. at the grills. I took mercy on Sam and fed him an overcooked wurst. He was quicker than a garbage disposal. Two bites and gone.

Tony came over for a burger refill. "Zak's got passes for a sneak preview of *Cujo* Saturday night. Wanna go?"

"Isn't that one of those Stephen King things?"

"Yeah. It's a killer St. Bernard. Pretty good book."

"I'll pass."

"Oh, I forgot. Mister High-Falutin' Lit here. Let's go see *Finnegans Wake Part Two* instead."

Tony never forgave me for picking *Passages from Finnegans Wake* at the Art Museum over *Escape from New York* at the Mayfield Flea Pit one Saturday night.

Dewey and Meg, sharing a glass of Wild Turkey, strolled over to the grill.

"You get to drive Omar to the field, Bud."

"Zak and Tony'll have to do it. They're parked in the road, I'm blocked."

"Good enough. Bob's taking a load in his heap and the rest of us can ride in Billy's truck."

"Meg's getting sloshed. She's starting to weave."

Meg took off a shoe and whacked me with it. She kicked my shin with her other pointy shoe.

"Jesus. I surrender."

"You better, sugar britches."

I rounded up our vanguard of fart-fans and we piled into two cars and lit out for Brainard Field.

BLAM

$\mathcal{P}$articipants and onlookers crisscrossed the grassy field on foot and bicycle. Dogs romped in the clover. A Kool-Aid salesman hawked grape bugjuice. There was a lot of obscene yelling, and one dorky kid lip-farted into a Mr. Microphone device.

Sam Simpkins, the moderator, sat on the edge of a flatbed truck, paging through applications. He was beetle-browed and ruddy. He looked like a counselor at a wilderness survival life-is-hell summer camp.

"What's the story on this pervert, Omar?"

"Guess he just likes the gas."

Zak found some shade to park in. Cicadas rasped in the dusty old elm grove. Local cops frowned on public beer drinking, so we had improvised our refreshments. Tony had mixed some Wild Turkey into a plastic bottle of Coke. He shook it up till it fizzed, then squirted a jolt into his mouth. He passed it to me and I took a slug.

"We should've brought a pail to puke in," Zak said.

Some of the farters congregated on the grass. They tried psych-jobs and gross-outs, tugging at each other's pants and ragging on each other. Omar did some squats and duck-walked like a sumo wrestler. He blowfished his cheeks. Trudy handed him a bottle of warm Mountain Dew. He gargled and spat.

There were sixteen contestants in two eight-asshole brackets. The reigning champ, Arnold Sorrento, was on the opposite side from Omar. This Sorrento kid, though only seventeen, looked like a nose guard on the Ohio State football team—porcine but muscular, with dim gray eyes. He wore a ragged blue sweatshirt with the arms snipped off to reveal his hamlike biceps and hairy pits. He ignored the other kids, jogging in place and pumping his elbows.

Meg's car, Bob's car and Billy's truck arrived convoy style, honking their horns. Omar was ticked off. "Quit bleatin', you crack-wipes."

It was 4:02, blast-off time.

Simpkins had a mike rigged up. "Let's get organized here, people. Welcome to the Fifth Annual Fourth of July Farting Contest. No corporate sponsorship accepted. We're still independent. We got sixteen top gas-passers lined up this year. This is strictly a junior event—nobody over eighteen, no hustlers, no ringers, no out-of-town shitbags. And we're on the lookout for   lady participants. This is a coed event.

Kids, if your sister can toot a few and she isn't too bashful, sign her up next year." This caused some titters.

"I'm gonna go over the rules...You got ninety seconds to get off six good farts. Judging's by sound quality, stench, and style. A low of zero for a total misfire, a high of ten for the ultimate cannon shot. Which we ain't heard yet in four years. I keep the standards high...Style's subjective, but I'll give you some hints—no mooning, no ventriloquist bullcrap, no ridiculing your opponent, no excessive strutting. And no back-sassing the judge. My scores are impartial and final. Any of this nonsense can get you disqualified. We want solid athletic farting here—that's the idea." He studied his papers for a moment.

"Okay. Two minutes to start. First up we got Bob Levy versus Kevin Colombini."

Kevin grinned one of his overbite specials. He spread his arms à la Tony Bennett and belched. Omar rapped him on the arm.

"I feel good," Kevin said.

"Break it off if it gets squishy," Omar advised. "Then just repeat 'cement-butt, cement-butt' over and over to yourself. It works."

The arena of battle was a pebbly circle where a playground whirler had once set. Simpkins perched on a deck chair at the edge of the oval, wearing a pith helmet, black boxing trunks and combat boots. Salt-and-pepper fur ran down his big bare belly. He had a gas mask at his feet.

Simpkins punched a button on his boombox and the Jimi Hendrix version of "The Star Spangled Banner" played in an ornery squall of feedback. There were fifty or sixty fearless spectators on hand, many of whom applauded the music.

Our contingent crammed together so we could share the Wild Turkey and Coke. Meg had brought another bottle of the same mixture. Lydia downed a swig and Danton guzzled a big swallow. O.T. polished it off.

"I hate drinkin' you all's spit," O.T. said. "Except for you, Lydia. You could spit up in the air and I'd catch it like a fetch ⬛ dog."

"Don't mind O.T.," Bonnie said. "He likes to impersonate white trash just for the art of it."

Lydia seemed unfazed, leaning against Charles. He stroked her arm. I could smell her perfume—*eau de* Discount Drug Mart.

Bonnie had her shades on, the ones with the pink butterfly wing frames, and her *Hee Haw* party dress of red, white and blue polka dots.

Simpkins called the first pair of farters forward. Bob Levy was a fat boy with a keg-sized ass.

"Kevin's in trouble," Omar said. "This guy farts so hard the draft sucks his underpants right up his ass."

Levy flapped his arms like a chicken-boy and cracked two loud farts. He jiggled his legs and let one that sounded like the mating call of a bull elephant.

Levy shut his eyes and grimaced. He squatted slightly and blew a low rumbler. He paused a few seconds, then blew another froggy rumbler. He went into a discus thrower's contortion and ripped his sixth and final fart.

Simpkins sniffed the breeze like a dainty and disdainful cartoon bulldog. "Nine on sound, six-point-five on aroma, eight on style. Twenty-three-point-five."

Simpkins's aide, Art, had a scorebook. He entered the score.

"Okay. You're up, Mr. Colombini."

Kevin padded down the slope into the pit. He struck a disco pose, arms arrowed, and farted softly.

"Mosquito poot," somebody heckled.

Kevin rubbed his mug. He cocked his scrawny banjo-butt and let a blast. He grinned proudly. Touching his toes with his ass outthrust, he popped two medium-loud farts. Unfortunately, his fifth fart was soggy.

Flamboyantly he walked around the arena on his hands, flipped himself prone, raised his butt pneumatically, and cut a whistling blast. Hands aloft, he exited the pit.

Simpkins cleared his throat. "Mr. Colombini, I give you a six-point-five on sound, a nine on smell—what the hell you been eatin', boy? And an eight-point-five on style. Twenty-four."

Omar pounded Kevin on the arms. "My man! The miracle asshole of '83."

"Hey douche nozzle, your wallet fell out," somebody called. Simpkins picked up Kevin's wallet from the dusty pit and tossed it to him.

Sorrento took his match with a six-bagger of hard, thumping farts, spaced ten seconds apart, with a total absence of embellishment. He won 22–16 over a demoralized sixteenth seed, who strained and gaped and almost dislocated his pooper.

"How you holdin' up, Meg?" Dewey said.

"My second husband Enos could waste the lot of these bums. That man could sit in a tub of water and play *Victory at Sea* with his ass muscles."

Omar's competition was a freckled kid named Barry Dennison. He wore bleach-stained cutoffs and a Def Leppard T-shirt. On his third fart the sound went from a whoosh to a splatter as he shat his cutoffs.

"Whoops. First disqualification of the day. Take a hike to the john if you can still walk, Mr. Dennison. Mr. Carew, you can treat this as a bye or go ahead and wail."

"I'm gonna blow 'Dixie.' "

Omar strolled into the ring. He turned his black hat around backward. He did two deep knee bends, then thrust out a fist and farted viciously. His next three farts duplicated Sorrento's spartan thuds. He squatted in slow-motion and cut a long, moaning fart. He rose up and nonchalantly let a final boomer.

"You die, Sorrento," he said as he left the ring.

Simpkins fanned himself. "That's a nine on noise, a nine-point-five on reek. The Pentagon's got a job for you in the germ warfare division, boy…And an eight on style. Twenty-six-point-five. Watch that taunting, though. Show Mr. Sorrento the respect due a champion."

Imperturbable Art sucked a lollipop.

There was a ten-minute recess between rounds. Dizzy from the heat and alcohol, I walked to the drinking fountain. I doused my face and rinsed out my gummy eyes.

A bandy-legged old man wearing a Spanky McFarland hat and walking a panting little terrier on a leash came up behind me.

"What's the commotion over there? Marble tournament?"

"Nah. Two midgets were giving a kickboxing demonstration and one of them just kicked the other's teeth out. Now it's a teeth hunt."

He gave me a scornful look.

"Excuse me, sir. I lied. It's actually a Christian rampage. We're making heathens eat firecrackers. That's those pops you heard. Pretty awful, but we have to do it. We had a vision."

"You take me for a total butthead, huh?"

"Yes I do, sir. We're all total buttheads. Let us kneel and pray." I sank to my knees on the sharp gravel.

"Get in a drug program before it's too late." The wily old geezer bent to drink. He filled his hat with water and let the tawny pooch lap some.

"Sir, let me caution you. A mixture of clothing dye, head sweat, and tepid water might cause a seizure in a small dog."

"Get outta my face."

"I warned you." I made a brief epileptic dogface grimace and walked back to the mob. What a woeful third-rate drunken cutup I was! The old guy had bested me.

"Round two commences. Kevin Colombini versus Joey Kowalski, the Polish Terror."

The crowd was getting rowdier—whistling and clapping and skipping flat rocks into the trees. Angry crows flew for safety.

"No rockin', people," Simpkins warned.

Where did Omar obtain his farting powers? Maybe from my Uncle Lou, my mom's older brother. He was a secu-   rity guard at Cape Kennedy now. I remembered his White Owl cigar and Limburger cheese ambience. He once ended a pinochle game with a single fart.

In the ring Kevin squatted and cut a good one. He did a few squirrelly Al Jolson moves and farted again. He aimed his butt at the horizon and let two capgun shots. Puffing his cheeks, he farted weakly and moistly.

"Cement-butt," Omar urged.

Kevin was bold. He stood on his hands and, quivering, blew a solid blast. He backflipped and strode out of the ring.

Simpkins gave him a twenty-three.

Kowalski spaced six even, concussive farts, bowed solemnly, and was awarded a 24–23 victory.

"Oh man," Omar said. "That Terror's a drudge. No pizazz at all. Rice and carrot farts! Kevin's burps smell worse than those farts."

Kevin toddled off to the pavilion and we glumly watched Sorrento rout his opponent, 25–19.

Omar's opponent, Ray Rhodes, was overmatched. Six exhausted poots and he was knocked crossed-eyed from the exertion. Omar climbed into the pit, did some Muhammad Ali backpedaling, and cut five good ones and one mushy dud, winning 23–15.

Simpkins plugged the pause with some fart lore. "People, this competition can be traced back to a bar bet in the spring of 1979. Fellow named Hank Terwilliger bet me ten dollars that he could fart twenty times in one minute flat...Well, I lost the bet but gained an idea. Farting is one of the cornerstones of our heritage. This is a bean-eating society. The pioneers probably cut millions of bean-and-cornbread farts on those cold prairie nights. Better than an electric blanket. They don't call America a melting pot for nothing. Think what melts in our bellies. What we eat is what we fart, and farting's an art."

Simpkins blew a hog-snuffling blast.

"We ever get a senior circuit going, I'm the man to beat. Sorry, Art. Got you at close range…Some call it vulgar. Hell yes it's vulgar. We're a vulgar country. Let the silk-sheeters go to France. Be gone!…A man that can't fart just isn't a man. Enough said. Let's have the first pair of semifinalists up here. Mr. Kowalski, Mr. Sorrento."

Sorrento whupped the Terror, 24–21.

"What a slug," Omar said. "Brown rice and green vegetables and cottage cheese."

Omar's opponent, Bobby Gonzales, shadowboxed in the sulphurous pit. He cut three solid dingers, then flew into the mountain: skkkeeewissshhh.

"Life is hard, Mr. Gonzales. But you're outta here. Mr. Carew, the option is yours."

"I hate to disappoint my fans, but I'll take the bye."

"Rabbit-ass!"

"Pauk pauk pauk pauk."

Omar wasn't happy. "I may not have six dry ones left in the chute."

"Five minutes until the final match. There will be a trophy presentation afterwards." Simpkins unveiled a statuette: a grinning plump satyr in the squat position. The runner-up got a soap-on-a-rope cherub.

Omar rinsed his gob with Mountain Dew and ate a mini-box of raisins for quick energy. He brushed his spiky, flyaway, multidirectional hair. He wiped his face with a towel. He put on his black racing gloves.

Sorrento went first. His initial fart was a cannonade. His second was softer and denser—some seepage evident at last. He frowned and scanned the crowd for snickerers.

His next two shots were noticeably weaker. Number five was snappy and number six was an artillery blast. Sorrento paraded around the ring bullishly.

"I score as follows—eight for sound, seven for odor, eight for style. Twenty-three. Mr. Carew, the stage is yours."

Omar ground out two grooves for his feet and went rigid and honked a fart. He duck-walked a few feet, shook his haunches like a wet cat, and cut a mournful blast. Something inside him was whining to get out.

#3 also had a whistling sound, but it was good and loud. #4 was a squealer. #5 was soft and expansive—a wheeze.

Omar paced a few steps in discomfort. He stopped. With a bombs-away grimace he let his ultimate fart escape: a hot stew of crap poured down his legs. The grungebag wasn't wearing any underpants.

"That's the last time I trust my asshole. I retire," he muttered as he limped past us. Kevin and Dewey went along with him to the pavilion.

"Live by the cheese, die by the cheese," Tony said.

"The winnah and still champeen…Mr. Arnold Sorrento."

Sorrento shook hands with Simpkins and Art and accepted his trophy. Farting goliath that he was, he'd need a big mantle.

"Uh, I'd like to thank my parents and Woody Hayes and General George S. Patton. And my trainer, Sleek Thompson. And, uh, our savior Jesus Christ for givin' me the power."

Two cops parked at the faraway curb watched us disperse. I imagined a paddy wagon full of fart-frolickers and cringed. Omar returned, wrapped in a Turkish towel.

"Washing your ass in the sink is a trip," he said to Trudy.

Sorrento shuffled over like a punch-drunk boxer and cuffed Omar on the ear and consoled him. "More grains, less dairy products."

"More brains, less body builder mags," Omar said.

Sorrento shrugged off the insult. He left with trophy in paw to visit the pavilion crapper.

"Wait'll he gets a load of the sink," Dewey said.

"Let's split this shithole," Omar said. "I'm hungry."

He wore the runner-up soap around his neck.

Holiday

Blues

---

*R*ayford had wursts on the grill when we got home. Jewel and Kaki, Rayford's girlfriend, were tossing ice cubes at Rayford, who deflected one with a meat fork.

"They're drunk and abusive again," O.T. said. He gripped Jewel's hand and made her drop some ice. Kaki, in a yellow bikini, lobbed another cube. Her navel puckered like a puppet mouth. Less hefty than Jewel, she was also a dog shampooer. Her own hair was a dirty-blonde shag cut. Jewel might have trimmed her with the shears and hosed her off and put her in a cage to dry.

"Ice fight." Kaki pitched a cube at O.T.

"Spank her, Rayford."

"You spank her, bubba."

Kaki hit Rayford in the head with a cluster of cubes.

"Goddamnit!"

O.T. encircled her arms and subdued her.

Kaki's Persian cat Herm was lolling on the grass at her feet, pawing dandelion fluff and watching it float away. Sam sprawled by the grills, eyeing the cat.

"Who won the big contest?" Jewel asked.

"Omar struck out in the bottom of the ninth with the bases loaded," I said.

"The little shit owes me five, too," Tony said.

"Good luck collecting it."

"Hey Kaki, okay if I play with *110* your pussy?" Zak said.

She threw some ice at Zak and stroked Herm with her bare toes. She tilted too far and fell off her chair.

"Kaki, eat some food. You're plastered," Rayford said.

I fished out three beers and passed two to Tony and Zak.

Kaki started eating Jell-O with a plastic spoon. She catapulted a spoonful at Zak.

Omar came outside wearing checked pants, suspenders and no shirt. He excavated a blob of Jell-O and sat down at the table to eat.

"There's a run on Jell-O at last, Bob," I said. "What'd you do, use hypnotic suggestion?"

Bob ignored my jibe. He dished out some Jell-O for himself. "You stumblebums want some Jell-O to go with your beer?"

"Yeah, we need some ammo to fight Kaki with."

Trudy and Dewey and Meg trooped outside.

"Omar," Dewey said. "I want you to maintain a tight butt for the rest of the day. You've put poor Trudy through enough."

"Quit tryin' t'brainwash my girl."

"Send him to military school," Meg said.

Dewey shook his head and chortled. "He'd turn 'em all into pacifists. Help me bring the melon balls out, Bud."

I hauled the big punch bowl and Dewey the smaller bowl. We set them on the table for the delectation of the gathered drunks.

Dewey put some Lefty Frizzell on the box for Meg. Charles took off his shirt and glasses and danced on the grass with Lydia. Dewey and Meg danced and he had his hands on the seat of her shiny-blue slacks.

"Let's call a truce and do-si-do some, Kaki," Zak said. "I bet Rayford only knows the Dirty Dog."

Kaki was too plowed to refuse. She staggered at first, but started dancing more gracefully as Zak ogled her knockers.

"We need women," Tony said. "I know I ain't dancin' with you."

"That's okay, 'cause I only dance with Jane. Why not ask Trudy? Omar only knows how to slam dance."

"We need to get drunk, then."

"That's a good plan."

I had two wursts for ballast, but boycotted the melon and Jell-O jubilee. Piss-poor desserts, they were. I went inside and found some coconut macaroons, which were stuck together in one big gummy symbiotic cluster.

Bonnie and Penny and Danton sat at the kitchen table drinking gin and papaya juice. I sat down and tried one.

"Bust me off a cookie, Bud," Bonnie said.

"Me too," Penny said.

I pried loose two macaroons and dealt them to the ladies.

"Now tell us your favorite book, Bud," Bonnie said. "We're taking a survey."

"You know what it is. *Death on the Installment Plan.*"

"I have to read that one," Danton said. "*Journey to the End of the Night* was a killer."

"I know Jewel's favorite is *Gone with the Wind*," Bonnie said, and Penny's is *V*."

"O.T. likes *Hot Crotch Nurses at Charity Hospital*," I said.

"What's Dewey's?"

"Probably *As I Lay Dying* or *The Sound and the Fury.*"

"I'm changing mine to *The Member of the Wedding*. *V* is too esoteric." Penny took another cookie.

"Not on campus it isn't. Those English department geeks worship Pynchon."

"Weren't you an English department geek?"

"No, I was a heretic. I had my own half-assed curriculum. I read a lot of Günter Grass and Céline and all the South Americans."

"That's where my favorite comes from," Bonnie said. "*One Hundred Years of Solitude.*"

112

"Good choice. What's yours, Danton?"

"Hard to say. I like this book *Many Slippery Errors* by Alfred Grossman, but some bastard stole my copy."

I took a dig at Penny. "What's the attraction of *Member of the Wedding*? Wasn't that a movie with Judy Garland?"

"Listen to this ignoramus. Try some other women writers besides Flannery O'Connor. You'll learn something."

"I read *Silas Marner* in high school."

"*Silas Marner* and *Wuthering Heights* don't count."

"Jewel will lend you some Rona Jaffe novels, Bud," Bonnie said. "And it wasn't Judy Garland in that movie. I know the little kid from *Shane* was in it. And Ethel Waters, I think. But I can't remember who played the girl."

"Patty McCormack."

"No."

The gin was starting to kick in, tickling my brain with its evil vapors. "Hey Penny, Jewel and Kaki challenged you and Lydia to a Jell-O wrestling match. Bob says it's okay to use his stock."

"What'd I tell you, Danton? Spare the rod and spoil the child."

"You know you love me."

"Do not."

"Jane loves me."

"She's probably in the arms of another even as we speak."

This bothered me enough so that I belted down another gin-and-papaya-juice cocktail. My head buzzed. I thought of a nasty reply—"You should join a coven, Penny"—but I didn't say it aloud. I could hear firecrackers in the distance. Suburban insurrection.

I stood up and abandoned the huffy literary circle. I felt like having a fistfight with somebody I despised—Dick Nixon or George Steinbrenner or

Donny Osmond. I felt poisonous enough to take on all three crudballs. Grind Donny's nose flat and bite Nixon's ear off and curb-kick George's tyrannical face.

Dewey came in and put a Patsy Cline record on as I was stumbling out. The backyard was completely shady now. The Burdette brothers wolfed wursts. Meg danced with Sam, whose fat pink tongue dangled out of his pink-and-black jowls.

"There's laws against that."

Meg ditched Sam, who thumped to the grass, and kicked me in the ass.

"The natives are getting vicious," Tony said.

"My head aches, my stomach aches, my heart aches. Now my ass aches... Trudy, you're the only woman at this gathering who isn't a beast."

Trudy gave me a big goofy grin. Omar sat next to her, eating Doritos and using potato salad for dip.

There was a steady parade of commuters to Billy's honeywagon. Everybody's kidneys were working double time. I strolled over and got inside and took a long easeful whiz. Back at the picnic site, I plunged my head into a tub of ice water.

At dusk Penny and Danton and Bonnie wandered outside, all looking stewed. Dewey switched off the remote speakers and let Omar and Trudy take over the stereo inside. Shortly we could hear a Troggs record playing.

Zak and Tony and I maintained our position at dog-level on the grass. A few lightning bugs winked on and off. Sam and Herm were about three feet apart on the lawn, both snoozing. Billy fetched more ice and Dewey replenished the beer tubs.

Something that Rayford said caused Kaki to go into a laughing fit which devolved into a coughing fit which petered out into erratic hiccups. Rayford rubbed ice on her neck to distract her, and as she smacked back at him her hiccups went away.

Dewey lit two candles and all the adults settled at the three picnic tables and soon the talk turned to sex.

SYMPOSIUM

BILLY: I ain't had a good piece of ass in a year.

KAKI: You need to sober up and join Weight Watchers, Bill. Or else we could run you over to the petting zoo and maybe you'll get lucky.

JEWEL: Who was the victim a year ago, blubbergut?

BILLY: Can't remember. It was dark. Might've been a sheep then.

RAYFORD: Did she bitch afterwards or bah?

BONNIE: I should've put some saltpeter in the potato salad.

ZAK: You think you're hurtin', Billy—look at us.

ME: Don't lump me in with you guys. I'll be cursed.

TONY: You're O for July, you stuck-up fuck.

MEG: You get me drunk enough, you might have a chance, Zak. You got any protection?

ZAK: I hate those damn things. All they do is deaden the good vibrations. You get done and you're stuck with a soggy balloon full of pudding on your wheezer. What're you supposed to do with it?

ME: Memorize where the wastebasket is before you start and flip it in that direction afterwards.

KAKI: Tuck it behind your ear.

MEG: Stick it up your ass and shit it out later, you pig.

DEWEY: Should I put the coffee on, Meg?

LYDIA: As long as we're delving into smut, tell everybody about your first blowjob, Charles.

CHARLES: Ah, we were reminisc- ing about our high school erotic experiences the other day…Anyway, this was in Ann Arbor, so I can't embarrass the girl too terribly.

MEG: As if it matters. You scuzzballs always blab every time some dumb dame gets within six feet of your goodies.

DEWEY: Easy now.

CHARLES: Hello, Melanie, wherever you are—and forgive me for what I'm about to tell…We were only sixteen. We were fooling around on her couch and Melanie smiles this impish smile and says, "How 'bout a blowjob?" and I say, "Sure, great, go right ahead." She gets my shorts down and she's touching me kind of tentatively—reconnoitering. I'm so excited I shut my eyes, I can't believe what's about to happen.

BILLY: That's the way it works with me. I can't believe some little cutie's actually gonna chow down on my poker.

CHARLES: I'm waiting and waiting and eventually I hear this "phew phew phew" sound and I feel a cool breeze on my business. Melanie's blowing on my dick—literally.

O.T.: Them Fruit of the Loom people should put a glossary and a diagram inside every pair of shorts. We could pass 'em on to the girls as a study guide.

ZAK: Did you straighten her out?

CHARLES: Nah. She was so cute and she thought she was being real bold. I didn't have the heart to criticize her.

JEWEL: Those things are kind of awkward t'put in your goddamn mouth. I'm glad O.T. ain't that big.

O.T.: Don't listen. She almost fainted the first time she saw it.

TONY: I got one that's pretty bad, if we're talking literal interpretations of oral sex. I was about thirteen and my friend Jimmy Sykes was walking home from school with me and he turns and says, "Wow, you shoulda seen my brother last night. I get up t'get a drink about midnight and he had his girlfriend on the couch and he was eatin' her pussy like a maniac…" I almost freaked. I wanted to ask him, "What'd you do, call the cops?" but I kept my mouth shut. I thought he meant "eating" like a cannibal. I never heard that expression before. It really messed with my mind.

PENNY: They should teach all the definitions for oral sex around sixth grade or so instead of handing out those polliwog pamphlets.

TONY: I could see the nuns with a pointer and a blackboard. "This is the clitoris, class. Touch it with your tongue and you'll fry in hell."

MEG: My old boyfriend Alvy always wore a bib during oral sex. Talk about a drooler...

O.T.: The trick is to get that little slip-slop spotless. Then it's *uhm-uhm-good.* What I do with Jewel is get her to soak in a tub full of bath crystals...They got flavors. They got a peach. That's the best one. Leaves that beauty tastin' better than cobbler. You'll wanna put some Cool Whip on it, it's so good.

JEWEL: You done kissed it for the last time, pardner.

O.T.: You know what they always say, Jewel—"The pinker the winker, the neater the peter." All's I'm tryna do is keep my peter neat.

RAYFORD: I get tired of those fruity douche flavors. I wish they'd come up with a nacho cheese or a ranch flavor.

BILLY: Sour cream and onion.

O.T.: Pass me two beers, Bud. I need a peace offering.

JEWEL: Beer won't do it. Let's dump these two losers, Kaki.

PENNY: Store this material, Danton. You can break it out if you ever tour Appalachia.

ZAK: I got one. Remember Dave Maloney, Bud? That skinny little bastard with the Martian ears? He missed school once and he was walking funny the next day, so I said, "What's wrong, Dave?" "Oh, my back hurts. I was laying on my bed the other night and I tried to blow myself, and I think I pulled my goddamn back out..." Could you see the note from his mother? Please excuse Dave because he wrenched his back yesterday trying to blow himself.

BOB: The worst misconception I had, I got from some fuckin' John O'Hara book. There was a honeymoon scene, and this guy refers to the screw something like, "I got all eight inches inside her." Made me feel like a stump-dick midget 'cause I only got six. Then that McKenzie report, or whatever it was, came out—turns out that ninety percent of all peckers are between $5^{1}/_{2}$ and $6^{1}/_{2}$ inches. Phew, was I relieved.

ME: Dig that ruler into your groin so it really hurts and you'll get an extra half inch, Bob.

BOB: Won't do me no good now.

MEG: My first husband Harry was a ten-percenter—and I don't mean on the long end.

PENNY: You always pick on Harry.

MEG: That man was so small he could jack off on a Ritz cracker without sloppin' any over the side.

BILLY: *Biggest* one I ever seen was Ted Purdy. We were down in an eight-foot hole, diggin' away, and Ted hauls out his diddler and pees straight up over the lip of the hole without rainin' one drop on himself.

LYDIA: Size is irrelevant.

PENNY: Hmmmmmm.

CHARLES: It's all in the strokes, folks.

ME: It's all in the feeling.

MEG: Put a lid on it, Mr. Loveitis.

ME: You cheap cynic.

DEWEY: It's not that cheap, Bud. The Wild Turkey outlay alone is draining our coffers.

MEG: Cash me in for some teetotaling New Wave tootsie.

JEWEL: He'll stick with you, Meg. We got all these dogs on a leash. Shit, I held out on O.T. for a week a few months back, and when I finally took pity and gave him some, he got so excited he rammed his head on the headboard of my bed and almost knocked himself silly.

O.T.: Here's what actually happened. I got a cramp in my calf muscle while poontatin' with old Jewel. My bad boy slid out when I got the heebie jeebies, and during the commotion old Jewel's goin' oh-oh-oh and tryin' to fit it back in, and the upshot of it is—I came like a bird dog in her hand. I'm writhin' in pain with this knot in my calf and she's got a handful of schmuckola she don't know what to do with.

JEWEL: I know what I shoulda done with it.

KAKI: Men and their dicks, what a routine. Craziest one I ever met was this guy Mike. He'd talk to his dick. Do it through the whole date. "Could be, might be, gettin' warm, she's dodgin' us, maybe later, down boy..."—all night long. He like apologized to his dick when I wouldn't go home with him.

MEG: Some men get too friendly with their own whangs.

PENNY: Tell us your worst blunder in bed, Bud.

ME: Do I have to?...This is terrible. I *like* Cissie and she was good to me in a time of need. I feel like a cad telling it, but what the fuck—we were in her dorm room and I was in the doggy position, which I wasn't too familiar with except in books and movies, and I was really, really drunk.

RAYFORD: Sounds familiar.

ME: Cissie had the lights out and I was poking around in the dark, basically...I hit the wrong opening.

O.T.: Signaled for a left turn and made a right, huh? Don't feel bad, Bud. It's happened to us all.

ME: Boy, was she shocked. I felt awful. I did a wheelie outta there...Don't say anything, Meg.

MEG: A moment of silence for Wrong Way Corrigan...Tell you the truth, if you're down in Kentucky you're lucky if the guy hits your snatch by accident. He's usually *aiming* high.

119

BILLY: Sometimes you hit paydirt, sometimes you hit just plain dirt.

RAYFORD: Stick with the squish, Bud. It's healthier.

O.T.: At least put some grease on that puppy's nose if you're gonna go huntin' in the dark.

LYDIA: The worst one I had was sex on acid. I kept flashing to Bob Hope and Milton Berle and Buddy Hackett. Those guys are supposed to be funny, but they're really sinister when you're fucked up.

CHARLES: Was Henny Youngman in there?

LYDIA: No. But Red Skelton was. Like a demonic version of Red Skelton.

PENNY: Do some of your stand-up sex stuff, Danton.

DANTON: I don't have that much. Ah, hell…Imagine a planet way out in the galaxy where beautiful women wearing Frederick's of Hollywood outfits are looking at magazines full of pictures of fat guys in bathrobes holding their dicks in their hands…Now imagine the waiting list for astronauts to that planet.

BILLY: Sign me up.

DANTON: Everybody ponders the meaning of life. What if God wrote a skywriting message across the sky—ATTENTION EARTHLINGS. LESS WORSHIPPING AND MORE FUCKING. OR ELSE…The whole planet goes into an erotic frenzy to appease God. Churches change their names. Our Lady of the Bloody Painful Thorns becomes Our Lady of the Vaginal Orgasm…Then God starts making flaky demands—DEFLOWER BROOKE SHIELDS IMMEDI-ATELY. Brooke goes underground. Posses of slavering vigilantes are on her trail…That's all I got on sex. I got some really sick restaurant humor, but everybody just ate…

PENNY: Do the God rap, Danton.

DANTON: I don't know if this'll elevate or lower our discussion, but here goes…God's sitting in his celestial lawn chair way up above the clouds, surveying all his pipsqueak creations and listening to all their prayers. Billions of prayers zapping in from all over the universe.

He's got his shades on, loose   clothes, a frosty one in his hand. He

120

takes a drink. He starts to blabber, "Look at that ant farm down there. Earth is absolutely my least favorite planet. I screwed up on the climate thing. I screwed up on the topography thing. I *really* screwed up on the pigmentation thing—I thought they'd *enjoy* all those different skin shades, but listen to 'em bickerin' and ravin' at each other. I definitely screwed up on the territorial thing and the meat-eating thing. Shoulda made vegetables taste better, but I was inexperienced, I was just putzing around...

"At least they domesticated a few beasts, but Jesus Christ—and I don't use my kid's name casually—Jesus Christ, do they have to slaughter animals by the *herd*? I know, I know...they taste good. I o.d.'ed on the taste-bud thing, too. Not to mention the breeding apparatus thing...

"So. It's depressing, but what do I do about it? Shitcan the whole planet in some crackpot biblical firestorm? Tinker with it? Nah. They figured out the wheel, gunpowder, asbestos, coffee filters. They came up with engines and refined gasoline. They got split atoms. They got the mother lode of irrationality. Let 'em make their own adjustments.

"Worst part of the job is, I have to process billions of prayers every damn day. I may be omniscient but I'm getting really sick of this earthling prayer filibuster. It'd wear anybody down. You really want to know my attitude toward earth and its discontents? I can sum it up in six easy words: You broke it, you fix it.

"Tough one, huh, my petulant little earthlings? Doesn't matter how vociferous you get. How *needful*. It's too damn many prayers to deal with. Hey, I don't want to get a cosmic callousness rap, so my policy is: Every *ten* billionth prayer, no matter how sniveling it is, I answer. I got an angel who totes 'em up—ding ding ding ding. When numero ten billion clicks in, some lucky slob gets bathed in the holy beacon of a miracle.

"It's getting close now. We're up to 9,999,999,999. This one's kinda garbled. An African dialect. A throaty rasp. Something about water...Okay. Skip it. I'll take number ten billion and one. Some jerk from Lakewood, Ohio, wants me to slip him a stock tip so he can buy a new car for his mistress. Her name's Tawny.

This guy's sweating Tawny's happiness quotient. Okay, pucker up, Bubba. Here's my advice. Buy three thousand shares of Didey Toys. Hidey, it's a Didey. They got some snazzy new dolls that are gonna be a raging sensation in the upcoming sell-or-die Christmas season...Pretty rancid way of celebrating my kid's birthday, Christmas. But what can I do? I had a big-shot religious leader who was number ten billion a few months ago. He prayed for general guidance, so I put a bug up his ass to cancel Christmas. Bums me out, I said, loud and clear. He woke up in a funk, convinced that he was possessed by Satan *impersonating* God.

"This planet jerks my chain so much that I can barely stand to watch it anymore. I like to turn my chair on the veranda and face the other direction. *Way out there.* Way past the reach of your puny telescopes. That's where the really nifty planets are. Zoomanus, for instance. Climate controlled, 72 degrees in perpetuity. No humidity, no bugs, no snakes, no lizards. Excellent array of fruits. Everybody's got smooth mahogany-colored skin. No awful white people to develop politics, slavery, war, and other earthling-type follies. The only earthling activity that the Zoomanians are hip to is a kind of mirror image rock 'n' roll. On Zoomanus Derek and the Dominos and Creedence Clearwater Revival and P-Funk and the Velvet Underground are still together, still jacking out new albums. No drugs, no back-stabbing, no contract squabbles, no ego fits.

"What else can I say? You're already envious and neurotic enough. Why should I tantalize you? Zoomanus compares to Earth as Aspen, Colorado, compares to Newark, New Jersey. You people will live in Newark forever...Phegghhh. We're up to 178,000 prayers already. Give it a rest. This is God—signing off."

MEG: That was good, sweetheart. Now to get the topic back to earthly screwing— if men could just screw as vigorously as they talk about screwing, all women would be smiling.

DEWEY: Who'd take care of all the crappy jobs and services? Men do most of the lugging and hauling jobs. Come home bushed at night, their balls dragging

122

the ground, and they're supposed to put on a championship sex display. That's too much to ask, Meg.

MEG: Excuses, excuses. What's the heaviest thing you lift, a record?

DANTON: We need a planet of total sensual leisure. All manual labor done by drones. Everybody has the time and energy to pursue their sensual proclivities to the max.

BILLY: Sign me up.

O.T.: You're already on the planet of lardass jerkoffs, brother. Can't be on two planets at once.

BOB: If you had an unlimited supply of nookie, you wouldn't look forward to it as much.

ME: Bullshit. You eat food every day and you never get sick of it. It makes your mouth water. Sex is ten times better than food.

BOB: Ten times better than steak and potatoes?

MEG: Bob, you *are* a potato.

LYDIA: Maybe I'll fix you up with my friend Cerise, Bob.

BILLY: How 'bout me?

RAYFORD: You're on your own, Goober. We'll mail-order one of them Filipino brides if you get really desperate.

ZAK: My dad had the best definition of the perfect woman—a rich, deaf-mute nymphomaniac who's a good cook.

MEG: Your dad's a worthless jellynuts, Zak.

DEWEY: Let's cease hostilities. Meg, you need a motherlovin' cup of coffee. Six cups…I'll admit it—men are basically worthless and inferior. We surrender as long as you'll be merciful.

MEG: There'll be a tribunal.

DEWEY: Just don't execute us.

ME: Comrade Meg will deprogram us.

DEWEY: Let us maintain our ▮▮▮ lovin' rights.

JEWEL: We'll consider it.

O.T.: Whipped again. Pass me a beer.

AUSTERITY

*T*he five couples, with Bonnie as their post-sexual den mother, went inside and switched to Wild Turkey and/or coffee, leaving Zak and Tony and Billy and me to chug the remaining beers afloat in their iceberg tubs. Bob had to hit the road in the morning, so he bequeathed us the melting Jell-O and hobbled home on gimpy legs.

On a trip to the honeywagon in the dark, Billy jetéed over a plant stake. We all decided to piss in the weeds like riffraff from then on. Sam humped up onto the table and gobbled the last two burgers, and no one had the energy to discourage him. In less than an hour we finished the beer and went reeling inside.

About midnight it started to rain. Billy suggested topless co-ed jogging to cool off, but got no takers. I made Tony and Zak promise to sack here for the night, so as to avoid car crashes. Then I broke out the tequila. Why not? Foolishness has its own momentum.

I suffered a small wound slicing a lemon, as it was hard to determine the distance between my finger and the peel. Bonnie bandaged it for me. Trudy's dad came to pick her up and stayed for a couple drinks. He was loose as a greased-ass goose and wasn't taken aback by all the drunkenness and dissolution.

"Julie Harris," Bonnie said out of the blue.

"Huh?"

"The girl in *Member of the Wed-* *ding.*"

"Ah, yeah. She was in *East of Eden,* too, wasn't she? Always played the ethereal tomboy." I wouldn't say "ethereal tomboy" sober, but Bonnie always accepted any diction—high, low or mediocre.

"That's her. Wore her hair short in the fifties and risked getting a lesbian rap."

Bonnie took a shot glass off the tray and helped us assault the tequila.

"Independence wasn't enough," Tony said. "We should've sailed over there in our goddamn armada and taken England from those hoity-toity twats."

Zak snorted like a pig with a head cold.

"Let me know when you have to puke, Zak, so I can double-time you to a commode."

"I'm cool." But he was giggling spasmodically and leaking fluid at the nose—definite pre-upchuck symptoms. *Twenty-one, and our behavior is so repetitive,* I thought. Reruns.

Trudy's dad Earl shook hands all around and left with his daughter, who carried a take-home bucket of melon balls and her empty beanpot. It rained torrents, drumming the awning and cascading down the gutters. I got up to pee and fell down on the rug. Everybody had a laugh at my anti-coordination.

When the rain let up at two A.M., the Burdettes and their dog-grooming lovelies left, also bearing the gift of melons. Zak and Tony scoped out the two couches. They kicked off their shoes like cranky little kids. Omar spread newspapers over them derelict style and they swatted them off.

Penny and Danton and Charles and Lydia stood on the wet driveway, puzzling out the logistics of leaving. Drunk as I was, I got Zak's keys out of his pocket and backed his jalopy into the soaked weeds so that Charles could squeeze his VW out.

In the headlights I saw Sam, muddy and bedraggled, trawling the front ditch for guppies or underwater knockwursts. Danton's blood-colored buggy eased out and was gone, sleek as a vampiremobile.

I pissed another quart and flopped on my bed. Somewhere around dawn the phone rang and I heard tromping in the hallway. As I drifted back asleep, the heavy sludge of a hangover brimming in my head, I heard Dewey pull out of the garage. I got up around noon, showered, popped three aspirin, and put the coffee on.

Zak and Tony were askew on the couches, groaning slightly. Omar sat at the kitchen table, his Walkman fastened to his big noggin, counting pennies into a mason jar with one hand and eating macaroons and melon balls with the other. The smell of coffee aroused the two groaners. They rubbed their sticky eyes and scratched their hair and trudged to the john to piss. Sword fight maybe.

We had a brunch of coffee and melon. Omar doffed his headphones and filled us in on Dewey's early departure. Returning to the construction site at three A.M., Billy had taken a corner too sharply and dumped a scatological mess on the highway. The deputy county sheriff, weary from working a late holiday shift and bleary from three hours of thwacking windshield wipers, was not amused. He caught Billy scraping wet shreds of shit onto the berm with a board, and slapped him in a holding pen with a gaggle of cherrybomb terrorists, drunks and thieves. Dewey chipped in on the bail, had pancakes with the Burdette clan, then went to open the store.

Omar screwed the lid on the mason jar and presented it to Tony. "Here's your fiver, Antonio. Last time I bet with a fuckin' gouger like you."

When Dewey got home that evening, we had a family powwow. New rules for the rest of the summer: a sensible diet and no hard liquor (a few maintenance-level beers on muggy days only). And he'd bought a plane ticket to Oregon for Omar, departing Monday.

"Any lip and I'll enroll you in the Junior Green Berets and make you listen to Christopher Cross records. Just go out there, eat your fruit salad and your lettuce salad and your rice balls, and enjoy it. And show your mom some affection."

"If I get the d.t.'s and go on a ▮▮▮ kill-spree, it'll be your fault, Dew."

"Just do what I say. *Once.*"

"Yeah, but what would Grace say?"

"Oh Christ." Dewey held his head in his hands. Omar was referring to Grace Slick, whom Dewey had dated once in his Berkeley days. It was one of many admissions he regretted.

We sat down to our spartan dinner—spinach salad, hard-boiled eggs, melon balls—and Omar glumly munched his wrinkly, crackling spinach and said, "Save me, Grace. Save me from this cuisine. Fry me up some meat to eat."

Five minutes later, stabbing a melon ball, he continued, "Did he try'n get funny with you, Grace? Go for tit the first time out? Is that why you ditched his scroungy ass?"

"Go get me that Ping-Pong paddle, Bud. I'm gonna whup his ass purple."

"Guess I'll have to tattle to the juvie authorities, Grace. Maybe they'll place me with a family that serves a decent meal. Like a pork chop and some mashed potatoes." Then he clammed up at last, torturing us instead with a disco Chipmunks album.

Part
Three

ALL THOSE
CHANNELS

*I*n the last two week of July I worked shifts at both Pellardi's stores. Store #2 was down in Weaselville, the near west side, with knife-fight mementos of dried blood in the parking lot, guys selling silk shirts out of the trunks of their cars, purse snatchers on skateboards, a whole whirling carnival of crime. We unloaded the trucks during store hours. *No one* would work there after dark.

I enjoyed Leppo, the motormouth stockboy, who was a tabloid monologist. "Don't live near no high-tension wires, Bud. My Uncle Ganooch did and he can't get no more'n two thirds of a stiff peter anymore. The buzz from the wires fucked him up...You know that orange coloring they put in Popsicles and shit like that? Same poison they dropped in Vietnam...All those Bigfoot sightings up in the state of Washington? They're all hippie draft dodgers tricklin' down from Canada. They been livin' in caves up there, playin' boo with campers and drunks...You know what the top three signs that you're turnin' into a   fruit are?..."

All that information, and Leppo could juggle four cartons of cottage cheese, too.

When I got home Friday evening, there was a big brown metal box on top of the TV. Dewey was all set to dish out a feast of steamed green beans, brown rice and sliced peaches.

"I figured we needed a sensory treat of some sort, so I took this special cable deal. We got the whole works—HBO, Showtime, Playboy..."

We sat in a semi-stupor, nursing our miserable glasses of ice water, switching from movie to movie. I looked at the guide for 8:00. HBO—*Fast Times at Ridgemont High;* MAX—*Humongous;* SHO—*Summer Lovers;* TMC—*Yes, Giorgio.* It was 8:45, so we sampled them all, kicking from California dopers to some acromegalic freak eating dogs on an island to Luciano Pavarotti trying to act suave to two gorgeous naked girls sunbathing on a Mediterranean cliffside—

"Whoa. Hold it there, Dewey." He clicked over to *Humongous,* where there were more nude vacationers. "Give me that damn thing."

Dewey chuckled. "Who's the driver here? Probably a lot of domestic violence fighting over the channel changer these days." He tossed me the remote.

I fastened on *Summer Lovers* and we watched the rest of it. I felt an oceanic tide of tenderness and lust. I was hard as a pipe inside my shorts and I squirmed on the couch.

"That's the kind of vacation we could all use," Dewey said. "We'll split up the girls. I'll take the blonde and you can have the foreign-exchange brunette."

"Oh no."

"I thought you preferred brunettes."

"Not this time."

We beamed in the Playboy channel—interview with a playmate. "I just love guacamole. And, oh, long bubble baths. And F. Scott Fitzgerald—he's my favorite." I pictured a tubful of flappers slapping bile-green bubbles.

"It's cold showers, celery sticks and Norman Vincent Peale for us, Bud...Switch over to the ball game."

"Meg on the warpath again?"

"Pretty much. She's in a bitter period. She jokes about her exes, but she's really pretty bitter. Trouble is, a forty-year-old woman who's a multiple divorcée—that's a woman whose bitterness has got a root system. Tough to dig that sucker out. I know she's got some legitimate gripes, but Christ, I wish she would just let it go…"

"Doesn't she mellow out with a few drinks in her?"

"Once in a great while. Most of the time, she just gets fiercer. I always have liked women who're pisscutters, but maybe Meg should pop a Valium every now and then."

Over the next week I watched *Fast Times* from start to finish three times. Two more lovely brunettes, though neither could match the dazzling blonde in *Summer Lovers,* which didn't play again.

Dewey and I agreed that the poor schnook jerking off in his fish-jockey uniform in *Fast Times* was the most realistic depiction of teenage sex ever put on film. I empathized with the kid completely. Watching a voluptuous dream-girl frisking in a water sprinkler would make anybody grab his joint.

Really bad movies became a comic endurance test, and we sat through a bunch—*Neighbors, Under the Rainbow, The Best Little Whorehouse in Texas, Seems Like Old Times.*

Physical labor curbed *some* of my horniness. On my one day off from grocery stocking, I dug up the compost pile and wheelbarrowed it to the flower beds and mixed it into the soil. Eschewing the lazy man's weed-whacker, I edged the entire border of the property by hand. I quaffed the last two Old Milwaukees. I wondered if Dewey was back-sliding at lunchtime, downing the odd pitcher of beer with his salad.

In bed that night I engineered a fantasy ménage like a porno daydreamer—Jane on one side of me (a pillow), the lithe blonde from *Summer Lovers* on the other side of me (another pillow). I was just a jerk cuddling two pillows, of course, but there was a strong current of romantic feeling.

I refused to stroke myself. I was saving my jism for Jane—a great gusher for our August reunion. My shoulders trembled—it was an unseasonably cool night. I pressed the pillows and sheet around me, but I couldn't shape them into flesh. There was just no substitute for the touch of warm skin. If I had any purpose in life, it was to be wrapped in an embrace with Jane, loving her. The texture, taste and aroma of her body were my spawning ground. I was a salmon swimming up a waterfall toward Jane.

Hopelessly insomniac, I got up and padded into the living room and turned the TV on at low volume. I switched from *Hell Night* (Linda Blair in peril again) to *Ruckus* (Linda Blair caught in a vigilante shootout) to *Endangered Species* (cattle mutilation thriller) to *A.N.G.E.L. of Heat* (Marilyn Chambers karate-fighting a midget). I stuck with *Endangered Species* as the least idiotic of the four, which broke our cable-movie rule—Dewey and I usually picked the *most* idiotic.

By the flickering of the TV I reread Jane's latest card. "I'm becoming a sea creature. Glorious ocean sunsets. One great storm front, too. Like the end of the world—lightning on the ocean, the inkiest clouds. Freddie made monster-mash noises when the electricity fizzled, and Mom had to swat him with a magazine. Went to Provincetown and ate scampi. See you in two weeks, Bud. I yearn for a good dumb joke and B.B. and everything else. Hope your mailman isn't some kind of handjob card-peeker. Love. J."

Both Linda Blair movies had expired when I checked back. I watched an exercise girl with frizzy, sizzled hair and an electric-blue leotard on ESPN for a minute. I watched Dick Cavett, fey and slightly mummified, interview Alan King on some unidentified channel. I watched Faye Dunaway indulge herself in some Germanic histrionics in *Voyage of the Damned* on Channel 43—a doozy of a character, both fragile and dominatrixlike. When a commercial came on, I clicked the infernal TV off and went to bed.

The sheets were cool, but I was hot with desire. I had my B-movie fantasy troupe for four A.M. company—Faye sprawled indolently on the left, eyeing me suspiciously; Linda in the middle, a cozy plump cuddler; Marilyn on my right, a little dazed and affectless, but she probably just needed some non-porno friendship and a respite from vicious midgets. Who's first? Hit it, Faye.

RETURN OF THE
SEA CREATURE

*I*n the last few days before Jane's return I kayoed my discontent and lust by working at Pellardi's *and* Dewey's shop. Charles and Penny each took a couple of days off for romantic excursions. I became the complete blue-collar automaton—stamping prices on Hamburger Helper, stamping prices on Duran Duran tapes. Somebody'd consume it all, then I could stamp a new batch.

Up in Oregon Omar was probably scarfing grapefruit salad and bellowing his way through Joan Baez singalongs. Dewey rescinded the alcohol ban to celebrate his birthday, and we went on a gin-and-Schweppes bender the last Friday of July.

Pellardi's #2 had been vandalized Thursday night and was closed for repairs. The rampaging vandals had turned the condiment aisle into a ketchup-mayonnaise-relish mudslide, they'd torn out wiring and smashed banks of fluorescent lights, they'd poured mounds of laundry soap on the floor and raced the floor waxer through it, they'd made Bil-Jac and marshmallow cream sundaes in the freezer case, they'd done something behind the bakery counter that only a pathologist could describe. Frieda the cookie lady just wrinkled her face and said, "Ick."

Thank God or Jehovah that I wasn't tabbed as a repair-crew grunt. In fact, Zak and I and the other stockhounds were suspects in the caper. The burglar alarm wasn't tripped, and Joe the manager muttered about disgruntled fuckhead employees crouching in the storeroom until lights out and sneaking out like goblins to wreak mayhem. I didn't give two shits. I'd saved $550 to splurge with, and was retiring from the grocery business on Saturday.

As we got loaded Dewey and I watched the Cubs game, then switched to a double feature of *Android* and *Forbidden World.* I wondered how Klaus Kinski, who

135

played the mad scientist in *Android,* ever begat Nastassia. Must have involved some alchemy.

Sunday evening Jane phoned. "I'm home."

I let out a deep sigh. "Oh baby, I'm overcome with joy. Are you okay and when can I see you?"

"Well, we're leaving for Nova Scotia tomorrow. Daddy's got a job as a consultant to the sardine industry. I guess I could fly by your place around eleven for a good-bye hug." Jane chuckled her happy frog chuckle. She could never stay deadpan long enough to pull a good put-on.

"You know, you and Freddie both have these sadistic tendencies."

"Freddie sends his love."

"When can I see you, baby?"

"I'll be over at eleven on the dot. You just get your rest and be ready for a tussle. I'm hyper-horny. One lousy lifeguard and otherwise I kept myself pure for you."

"Give me his name and address. I'll have him maimed."

"Giorgio. He lifts weights. Really a yummy body. You better hire an army." And she crumbled into more chuckling.

"You sure this wasn't some big fat butterball of an opera singer? Did you take a balloon ride?"

"No sir. No balloons. Muscles all the way."

"I'll see you at eleven, baby. I love you."

"Love you too, you muscleless thing. Bye."

"I'll show you the only muscle that really counts. Bye."

I was euphoric. Unemployed again, yet flush with spending money. My stomach hard from labor. My sperm reservoir at record level. And Jane was less than two miles away.

I went to my bedroom at midnight and listened to Big Star's *Third* through my headphones. It was my favorite record, and even the darkest songs were bene-

136

dictions that night. It was always best to listen to Alex Chilton's voice in the darkness, all raw desire and confusion and pain and immense pleasure and transcendence. I fell asleep afterwards like a happy child, wishing that my mom was there to square the blanket and kiss me.

The next morning I cleaned my room and went through my ritual body-hygiene drill. Must taste good in case Jane gets the munchies. I lectured my schlong, like the palooka whom Kaki had dated, "Go slow. No epileptic fits. No scattergun blazing away."

I squeezed fresh orange juice and toasted two bagels and set out some marmalade. 10:55. I poked my head in the freezer to cool off, and that's where I was when Jane rang the doorbell.

Frosty-headed and giddy, I went to let her in. She wore an orchid-patterned sarong and white sandals. Her tan was as rich as caramel. And to shock me she'd cut her hair short.

I took her in my arms and kissed her.

"What'd you do—freeze yourself while I was gone?"

"Cooling my brain."

"Do you hate my hair?"

"Your hair's beautiful and you're beautiful."

"You sure?"

"A Polynesian princess."

Jane scoffed, but she squeezed my hand tightly and leaned against me. I slid my other hand around her waist.

"I smell orange pulp. Got anything good for me?"

"Juice and plenty of it."

I led her to the couch. The hell with breakfast—that was for civilized types. I needed to gorge on love immediately. I kissed Jane's neck, easier to get at now. I kissed her sun-pinked seashell ears. Then 137 back to her lips. I felt the shape of her waist, its perfect curve. Workmanship. I stroked her calf up to her thigh, the silky fabric of her gown brushing my wrist, making the hairs tingle. My stomach was a-gurgle, my blood racing.

Jane wriggled gracefully sideways and back and was out of her sarong. She wore blue panties and a blue half-bra that showed the upper swells of her nipples. My head was defrosted now, my hair steaming. I slid her panties off, and got shock #2. Her wedge of pubic hair was drastically trimmed, streamlined.

"Jeez. Some barber up in Massachusetts went wild."

"Mom said I was showing too much bush through my bathing suit. So I trimmed it."

"Damn. I bet every bather on the Eastern Seaboard wanted to commit hara-kiri after you bushwhacked yourself. Men love that seaweed streaming out of a bikini bottom."

"Less is more."

I lay my head between her legs and kissed the insides of her thighs. I kissed her pussy. Still delicious. I let my hands play above, palming and caressing her taut breasts as I licked her. She shifted her hips and made low catfight noises. I followed the motion of her center with my persistent tongue until my heart and head and body spun with love.

The couch cushions kept sliding and I had my feet draped over an end table, nudging a lamp. I hated to interrupt our lovemaking, but bed was definitely more comfortable. I was a slob for comfort. I carried Jane into the bedroom. I kissed her breasts and mounted her and as I plunged into her I felt a total easing and flushing of my nerves. Home at last, swimming in friendly waters.

Much later, we had our orange juice and our crusty calcified bagels. "You do these with a flamethrower?" Jane dug into the marmalade pot with her fingers.

I changed the sperm-bombed sheets and we lay kissing and talking on the fresh, cool sheets.

"Remember Marge? My roommate from sophomore year who saw you naked that time? She's coming up from Baltimore and we're renting a cabin at Lake Piney. It's out in Geauga County. Don't panic now. You're invited. We're renting two cabins—one for us and one for Marge and whoever she can scare up locally. You'll come stay with me, won't you Bud?" Jane touched my scrotum coaxingly.

"Are you kidding? I'd go to hell to be with you, baby. Isn't Marge a bit of a stick-in-the-mud, though?"

"Oh you barely even met her. You'll have clothes on this time, it'll be more cordial. She's loosened up quite a bit. She even dated a soul brother last semester. I was proud of her. Her taste in music is the pits—Rod Stewart's *Foolish Behaviour* album, stuff like that."

"Wow, even worse than yours."

Jane increased the pressure on my nuts. "Watch it. Just because you dislike Joni Mitchell and Kate Bush, you persecute me."

"I do not. I can listen to about five minutes of Kate Bush per year and be perfectly happy. You just need to expand your listening habits. Drop the waifs, add some beasts. I'll borrow Omar's Motorhead tapes."

"Where *is* Omar? Are we safe with the door open?"

"Dewey packed the little snot off to Oregon till Labor Day. The house is so peaceful. It's blissful."

"I kinda miss him. He's a firebrand."

"A fire hazard."

"Marge's driving up here Friday and we're heading out to the lake. Are you sure you can come? Dewey doesn't need you at the store?"

"Huhn-uh." I kissed Jane's caramel tummy. I eased her onto her side and stroked her back and held her buns, so round and white. I wiggled down in bed and kissed each warm cheek.

"Ah-ah-ah. No more sneak at-139 tacks on my ass. I'm not ready for that."

I smiled, my lips a millimeter from her luscious butt. "Let me know when you *are* ready 'cause I'll be in like Flynn."

"What's the attraction of somebody's asshole?"

"The location, for one thing. It's right between your beautiful cheeks. And it's not *somebody's* asshole. It's yours. Sweet Jane's."

"Please respect my right to anal privacy."

"You know I will. You'll come around, though."

"Don't be too sure." Jane was blushing and smiling—an adorable girl. I kissed her lips and held her. Her hair was sleek and compact, not so luxurious to stroke now, but more of her beautiful face was open to touch. I basked in her beauty. I'd love her bald as a baby robin.

I hit the PLAY button on my tape deck. I had the Velvet Underground's *Loaded* tape cued to "Sweet Jane." Lou Reed let it rip, and before the song was over I was inside Jane again and the motion of my hips was a kind of language, saying "I love you" over and over and over. And with her own strong hips, in her lover's Esperanto, Jane replied "I love you" to me.

You Call This
a Lake?

*B*ack on the weed, huh?" I said to Meg, who sat cross-legged on the couch, one long freckled leg jiggling as she scowled and smoked up a storm.

"Oh you're so pure, you're so addiction free, Buddy boy."

I rummaged through the refrigerator for a beer and found a lone Pabst in the side pocket. Dewey ambled in, his hair slicked back, his seersucker suit baggy. "Watch out, Dew. She's like a scorpion tonight—all stinger."

"I look like an encyclopedia salesman with a wasting disease...Whadda ya think, Meg?"

Meg squinted and exhaled. "Ah, I'm used t'men lookin' like dicks by now. Let's hit the goddamn road."

"Hey Bud, I hate to ask, but Penny's going to Columbus tomorrow and Saturday. Danton's got a gig down there. Can you give me some hours the next two days—through the afternoon, anyway? You can get out to Jane by early evening."

I groaned inwardly, but said, "Sure, Dew."

Meg groped his baggy-pants ass as she followed him out and Dewey chortled. "I think I overdid this diet thing. Let's go for sauerbraten and red cabbage."

"Don't get wise."

"Don't get drunk and start robbin' 7-Elevens," I called.

I locked up the house and drove over to pick up Jane. We were going to see *Monty Python's the Meaning of Life* at the Mayfield Discount Pit. In front of the theater a barefoot man with a large egg-shaped head pat- *141* rolled back and forth with a sandwich board draped over his back. WORLD ENDS 8-8-83 AT 3:38 P.M. GET YOUR KITCHEN IN ORDER NOW. 38 JAKE.

"Why the *kitchen*?" Jane asked.

"Ask 38 Jake. At least we got two more nights of funnin' left. You be 38 Jane and I'll be 76 Bud."

With its liver-ripping rasta surgical teams, topless vigilante mobs and tidal-wave puking, *The Meaning of Life* was a pretty grueling comedy, not a great make-out movie. I drove Jane home and we sat on her porch and fondled each other's knees and kissed chastely till midnight. Ellie peeked through the curtains at us and turtled her head back when she saw me turn toward her. When I got home, Dewey and Meg were frolicking in his bedroom, Meg squealing directions or threats or a combination of both.

I felt happy and serene. I let Ives's *Three Places in New England* pour through my headphones. Then the Mozart *Haffner* and *Linz* symphonies, which I'd forgotten I owned, an old Otto Klemperer record from the sixties. I drifted asleep without a worry in my consciousness.

Friday at the store was hectic. Everybody was buying the Police's *Synchronicity* album. An old lady in a bonnet cleaned out our Rick Nelson section. A biker bought some Suzi Quatro oldies. I sold Bob Marley, Graham Parker, Ry Cooder, Devo. I wouldn't have been surprised if Jimmy Hoffa had bopped in to buy a MC5 album.

Jane called at 5:00 and said she and Marge were off to the lake, and they'd hold supper for my arrival. At 6:30 I drove home, showered, packed my kit, and sorted through my tapes to pick a few special favorites. Zak and Tony pulled in the driveway as I was stowing my shit in the car, and I had one beer with them. I gave them a Friday night pussyhunt pep talk—maybe sympathetic Martian nymphos would kidnap them and perform orgasmic experiments—and then split for the country.

It was hot and muggy as I headed east, the sky part smog-heap and part inferno-sunset in my rearview mirror. Geauga County was rich in forests, apple orchards and farms. Cool air blasted in as the traffic thinned on the darkening highway. I had an old Bob Dylan tape playing, *Blood on the Tracks.* Some kids wearing cowboy hats pitched apples at me, but I breezed past them. In a twilight pasture a stallion had his schnozz up under a mare's tail, and she whisked her tail back and forth coquettishly as he inhaled her goodies. Uhmmm-uhmmmm. I know how that horse felt.

It got too dark to see Jane's hand-drawn map. I pulled into a roadside tavern, Slugger's. They were doing lackluster business for a Friday evening. The barmaid was arm-wrestling some old codger and she whooped as she downed him. The friendly bartender looked like Chill Wills—string tie, snowy hair, jowls and all. He helped me to pinpoint Lake Piney, sold me an 85¢ draft (I was thirsty as a motherfucker), and tossed in a maroon pickled egg as a Welcome Wagon gesture.

"Watch out for that Buster LaRoca. He's a pissant...I hope you're not an investor, son."

I waved as I left. I had no inkling who Buster was. Some parking lot panhandler or hitchhiking loony?

It was pitch dark when I found the lake—a wood-burned chunk of pine nailed to a tree at the mouth of a rutted dirt lane, LAKE PINEY →. Smoggy clouds masked the floating moon. I drove over crunchy gravel as I neared the line of cabins. I spotted a dusty Toyota with Maryland plates by the light of a pumpkin-colored Japanese lantern.

Jane and Marge came out on the porch and stood slapping at bugs. When I got out with my bag, mosquitoes strafed my face. It was still warm and humid and dead calm. I could smell pine needles and brackish water and something as powerful as cat piss.

"It's the Holy Land for bugs," Jane said, shooing the skeeters from my face. "Marge, you remember Bud. Or at least parts of him."

"Hi Bud."

"Hi Marge."

With no further fanfare we went inside. Bare wood floors. A table painted mint green with three hard mint-green ![143] chairs. A flaming-orange beanbag chair. A wicker cornucopia fuzzed with dust and grease. A small kitchen equipped with appliances of 1948 vintage. A dysfunctional fireplace—a cement block on the andiron with a shirt cardboard taped to it: NO CAN USE in yellow Magic Marker. Above the fireplace was a painting—"The Last Supper" with all the apostles replaced by cartoon dogs à la Goofy.

"Well, at least we haven't fallen among devout Christians. Otherwise, just like the brochure said, huh?"

"There was no brochure," Jane said. "Wait'll you see the lake."

"It's a small pond with rotten cattails and a few geriatric ducks," Marge said. "Approximately as clean as the Ganges."

"You had to go and spoil it. Bud and I were going to take a moonlight stroll."

"How's the bed? Or do we just get a cot?"

"The bed's surprisingly comfortable."

I dunked my face in cool water to assuage my mosquito bites, and we sat down to eat. Marge was the chef-wizard—scallops and stir-fried vegetables and rice pilaf and hot rolls. Jane could barely cook a grilled-cheese sandwich. I uncorked the wine and toasted our surroundings.

"It's wretched, but we love it." Clink. "What's the other cabin look like?"

"Take a wild guess."

"Fire-engine red table and chairs," Marge said. "A hassock that looks like it got dropped out of an airplane. The painting above the no-can-use place is the St. Valentine's Day Massacre—pooches in zoot suits with tommy guns blazing."

"How many cabins are there?"

"Fourteen."

"That means the owner spent at least a hundred and forty bucks furnishing them altogether. Pretty low upkeep, too."

"Wait until you meet Buster."

My stomach queased. "He the caretaker?"

"Does it look like anybody takes care of this shebang? His mother owns it, going way back. She looks about eighty. I think they've been entrepreneurs out here for decades. He had us over for a beer and he was pitching bullcrap a mile a minute. I think he's got the hots for us, too."

Marge moaned and rolled her big brown alert eyes. She was a tall honey-blonde with wide shoulders and a cannonball ass. A semi-attractive bruiser.

"Tony and Zak may visit Sunday. Marge can pick out a bodyguard. Or take the matched set. They're a coupla Vikings."

"Goddamnit, Bud. Did you have to invite those two stooges? What ever happened to your friends from the baseball team? Or your Athens buddies?"

"I didn't *invite* them. What was I s'posed to do, sneak up here incognito? Zak and Tony pussyfoot around you, anyway. They're *afraid* of you."

Jane made exasperated bullfrog noises. "Convicts in the slammer are always looking for pen pals. Try some of them."

"Okay, I'll check out the Ohio women's facility. Where is it?...This dinner is great, Marge. Congratulations."

"Jane helped."

"Yeah. I sliced the peppers and mushrooms."

"I could go for a dish of white-chocolate mousse."

"Well, you're shit out of luck."

I think Jane was showing off to Marge, doing an acerbic number on me.

"There's more wine," Marge said. She darted a glance of complicity at Jane.

I let them steer the conversation to their University of Pittsburgh friends as I got quietly drunk. We were well into the third bottle of wine and examining a big ochre flying beetle when the screen door rattled in its frame.

"Duck and cover. I got three beers with your all's names on 'em."

Buster blotted out the porch light. He hulked into our cabin, smiling like a big shit-eating hedgehog. Short, kinky, dirty-blond hair and a thick, compressed neck. A pendulous gut and bandy legs. He wore butterscotch-colored Bermuda shorts smeared with charcoal and BBQ sauce and a T-shirt with I HATE EVERYBODY CEPT MY MOM stenciled on it and two alligator-faced caricatures embracing below the motto.

"Splendid digs and a bucolic setting, hey?" The fucker smiled broadly. "You mus' be Bud. I'm Buster." He gave a palm-crushing handshake. "You chaperonin' both these cuties or what? I like t'know the ins 'n' outs of these three-way arrangements."

"Just Jane."

"And Marge goes beggin'? You must be the last monogamous fool on the face of mother earth. That's not a criticism now. Just an observation from Buster."

As we finished our wine Buster drank all three beers in rapid succession. Marge wearily broke out a fourth bottle of wine and I uncorked it.

"I hear you're a literary tycoon, Bud. We get our share. Had Richard Brautigan for a night and part of a day once. I believe old Louis Bromfield cut through here on a sojourn way back when. Stopped to dip his hankie in the lake and apotheosize the view."

"It's a wonder Mickey Spillane never shot a beer commercial up here," Marge said.

"I don't write, Buster. I'm just a reader."

"No shit! He reads but he don't write. I got it wrong then. That's permissible, though. Hell, I need loyal readers. Bring him over tomorrow morning, Jane. I might give a dramatic reading or two. A century from now they'll be doin' *An Evening with Buster* on Broadway. I can outwrite-outbark-outgrowl-outbone any pantywaist writer on the planet." He laughed with gusto at his own dumb boast.

"Maybe Sunday. I have to work tomorrow."

"A wage slave! Ain't that a sharp stick in the heinie. Most disagreeable four-letter word in the language—*work*...Let me ask you this then. You're a worker, you're a consumer. You ever partake of a rutabaga? Boiled, mashed, anywhichway? Ever have knowledge of a rutabaga?"

"Nope."

146

"Ever read a Henry James book?"

"I know him a little better than I know rutabagas. I've read *Daisy Miller* and *Washington Square*. He's more Jane's kinda writer. All those semicolons wear me down."

"No endurance, huh? Soft in the belly. Well, good for Jane. Good for her...I favor James a lot. 'Course this twentieth-century shitstorm'd be too much for Henry to deal with. He's better on your horse-and-buggy situations."

"Buster," Jane said. "My eyes are starting to droop. One more glass of wine and let's call it a night."

Buster cackled and seized the wine bottle. He filled his own glass to the brim, then gave us each a tiny trickle—one, two, three.

"Sure thing, honeybuns. I'll guzzle the big one here, and let you kids taper off. You and Bud wanna snuggle up. I gotcha. What I could do is take Marge here outta your hair. Grab us a six-pack and shuffle next door. Hell, I popped a whole double load of popcorn for Ma a little while ago. If she hasn't pigged it all, we'll have us a snack item."

"Buster..." Marge paused. She frowned. "I got a sinus headache. I got a heat rash. I drove almost twelve hours today. Let's postpone our beer-and-popcorn bash. Till, say, about nineteen ninety-seven."

Buster puffed out his cheeks and whooshed a gust of laughter. "I'm in pisscutter heaven. Fit me for wings. I love these women. Don't turn 'em against me now, Bud. I'll see you girls in the morning. Soon as Bud hauls ass to his job, trip on over and dunk a doughnut with me. I'll bag Ma up 'n get her outta there...nineteen ninety-seven, ain't that the drizzlies?"

He crushed his three empty beer cans flat, palmed them, and boomed through the screen door. He poked his head back in and said, "Put some ointment on that rash. Or maybe some of our lake mud. It's got the magic healing properties. Cured Ma's bum-rash pronto."

He slammed the door shut and *147* lumbered away in the night.

"Skip down to the lake and scoop up some mud for Marge, Bud."

"Quit it, Jane." Marge showed her big white choppers as she whinnied with laughter. I thought the inevitable drunken thought: how would this formidable girl be in bed?

We said goodnight to Marge, and she went next door. Jane and I brushed our teeth side by side in the bathroom (more of a cubicle than a room) and got in bed. Jane had brought her blue sheets and her feather-stuffed pillows from home. The bed was wide and firm—an aberration in the Lake Piney scheme. I was woozy from too much wine. I let a belch that tasted of toothpaste, soy sauce and pickled egg.

"Jesus! Whatever that is, we didn't serve it for dinner. What a sewer mouth."

"Pickled egg. Sorry." I fitted my numb body against hers. "Like the song says, baby, I'm too drunk to fuck."

"What a dud." She tickled my pecker. "That one of Omar's songs?"

"He wishes...It's a Dead Kennedys song...God, is my head buzzing."

"I bet God is ignoring all complaints from this cabin. Wait here." I thought of Danton's God rap and muttered a prayer, hoping to hit the ten-billion lottery. Make me sober, God. Right now.

Jane sat beside me with a washcloth full of ice and pressed it to my forehead. She stroked my chest with her warm hand, then with her icy hand. My nipples stiffened and she kissed them. Rivulets of ice water ran up into my hair and down my chin and neck. Jane skimmed her tongue down my stomach and took my wine-stupefied dick in her mouth. I cast the icy washcloth onto the floor. Gradually my nerves awoke. I erupted. I stroked Jane's face as she made small laps and swallows like a bird at a birdbath.

"That makes up for me being a bitch before, I hope."

"You weren't. You can always say whatever you want with me, baby. Let me lick you now."

"You're still drunk."

"Just a petite sweet. Just a taste."

"Sober up first." She tapped my lips lightly.

I embraced Jane sleepily. "I love you completely, Jane. No more eggs, no more wine." A breeze nudged the gauzy window curtain, and I was asleep.

SATURDAY

CALM

*J*ane and I had spent the night together no more than a dozen times—two weekends in Athens dodging my scurvy and lascivious housemates and four weekends ensconced in her room in Pittsburgh. Waking up next to Jane, I felt an immediate surge of tenderness, even as the buzzing alarm clock struck a rimshot off my hangover/headache. I caressed her hip and extricated my other numb arm from beneath her back. I slid the sheet down, exposing her ass. I was too cowardly to kiss it, though.

I berated myself as I navigated away from the bed, bumping my shin on the door frame. In the booth-sized john I washed my mungy-tasting mouth out and brushed and gargled. The shower, designed to hold a midget, smelled as moldy as a root cellar. I dressed and snuck back to kiss Jane goodbye on the shoulder. I swallowed an aspirin-and-tap-water breakfast. I went out to the car, coffee-less and disoriented but not unhappy. The car was a-stream with dew and a daddy-longlegs spider slewfooted it down the hood.

Across the way a stooped old lady in a pink housedress and a sun hat the size of a sombrero was hosing the concrete patio at the side of the ramshackle house. When I pulled my creaky car door open, she straightened her back and glared at me. Madame LaRoca in flesh and spirit.

I taxied past the lake, which was indeed a combination duck slum and cesspool. There was a pathway of festive candy-colored gravel around the open end. A tree with pustulelike white berries drooped its branches over the far shore. Cattails and mixed sewer weeds gave the ducks some privacy to boat around in. Beyond the pustule-tree was an old barn the muddy gray-brown shade of a hornet's nest. Good place for a dinner theater—*Marat/Sade* and tuna noodle casserole.

I did my shift and Dewey liberated me at four. I hit the liquor store and splurged on four $9 bottles of wine. I stopped at the house to shower and grab an electric fan (a bug discourager as well as a coolant) and fired out to the lake.

Jane and Marge sat in their bikinis on the porch of Marge's cabin. Marge was sumptuous and a bit intimidating—she must go about 5′10″ and 150. Jane wore a very brief scarlet bikini, one of those butt-cheek-flaunting European jobs.

"You womens lookin' wunnerful dis ebenin'." I kissed Jane. "I owe you make-up whoopie galore tonight, baby," I said softly in her ear.

"I'll say."

I stowed the wine and the fan in our cabin, put on my cutoffs, and picked my way barefoot to Marge's stoop.

"Watch out for ringworms and chiggers and cooties," Marge said. "The entire insect world may be represented in the local dirt."

Jane chuckled. "The wide, wide world of bugs. You should've seen these little black scooters when I picked up that wet washcloth this morning."

I remembered what had made me discard the icy cloth and I had to shift my legs to give my erection more room to stretch in. "Speaking of pests, has Buster pestered you much today?"

"He dropped off a box of apples and a poem for Marge, but he only stayed a few minutes. Today's his deadline."

"The cops after him?"

"No," Marge said. "He writes this local supermarket giveaway rag. He does social commentary, restaurant reviews, movie reviews, concert reviews. A ghastly comic strip that looks like an autistic did it in crayon...Uses eight different names. His mom handles all the advertising and the personals—*six pages* of weirdos and dunderheads pining to meet each other in the current issue."

"Is this his Jamesian project?"

"Oh no," Jane said. "He's got novels, short stories, reams of poetry. He's got a screenplay going about Ohio cannibals."

"Sounds good."

Marge groaned. "It's called *People Jerky*. He's got these guys eating Stove Top stuffing and cranberry sauce with the people meat. Trust me—it's awful."

"He's hard to please when it comes to anybody else's movie. Check these out." Jane folded the paper to the capsule movie reviews and passed it to me.

BOBO'S LOUNGE   SHROPSHIRE DRIVE-IN
HAPPY HOUR 11 TO 11 $8 A CARLOAD
FREE PEANUTS EVERY MONDAY   BLUE THUNDER
PIKE ROAD & 303   FIREFOX

Now Playing Locally

Eugene Vorkapich—Resident Critic

FIRE CITY FOUR CINEMA

Porky's II: The Next Day (No *) For inbred Floridians and people who eat their
    own boogers only.

Superman III (½*) Too much pomade on Supe's hair and Richard Pryor doesn't get to cuss.

Psycho II (½*) No good in color. Norman Bates pooped out.

Krull (No *) Wizards and flying doodads and junk.

FALLS TWIN

Local Hero (**) Cranky Scottish whimsy. Pretty good when they serve that bunny they rescued for dinner.

Staying Alive (¼*) The snooty rich dancer is good for laughs. Directed by Silicone Stallone. Hey Sly, how come no Burt Young as a choreographer?

SHROPSHIRE DRIVE-IN

Blue Thunder (**½) Lots of shooting.

Firefox (*) Not enough shooting, too much Clint in a helmet.

FIRE COUNTY EXTENSION COLLEGE SERIES

The Bitter Tears of Petra Von Kant (No damn *) Like Peppermint Schnapps Night in the sixth rung of Hell.

"Buster reminds me of Chip, the critic in our campus newspaper. Sophomoric to a crisp. Wonder where he matriculated... What's the restaurant review like?"

"Needless to say, he doesn't like the local food."

"Show Bud the poem, Marge."

Marge unfolded a tablet page and handed it to me.

ODE TO A BIG BEAUTY

Now some like their
Split tails tiny
With hair so fair
And eyes so shiny

I like my women big
With many a proud pound
Like a Cadillac rig
Full and rich and round

To Marge
From Buster LaR
8-8-83

"This could be a sign of universal destruction. Remember 38 Jake?"

Jane laughed. "Well, Buster himself belittled it. Said it was an 'occasional' poem. Imagine how Marge feels."

"Just call me Cadillac Woman."

"By the way, Mister Moneybags, you get to take us to dinner tonight. And you get one beer or glass of wine tops." Jane's bare toes brushed my knees.

"Oh yeah? You been possessed by the spirit of your field-hockey coach or something? Three beers or three glasses of wine. Goblets."

"We'll see."

"Maintain his discipline." Marge *153* swiped me with her bare toes, too.

"His daddy never spanked him enough."

"Mom knocked the hell out of me once."

"What'd you do?"

"We were having a picnic and my Aunt Tess was sitting across from me. She had these amazing big old titties, and I decided to tiddlywink a green grape into her cleavage. Spur of the moment idea. Unfortunately, Mom happened to look right at me as I let the grape go. Boy, did she go wild. Got me down on the grass with her knees on my chest and slapped me stupid."

I sat on the bottom step of the porch with my head on Jane's lap. She massaged my scalp and tugged my ears. I kissed her knee.

"I told you he was hopeless, didn't I, Marge?"

Buster's yard in daylight was something to see. It was clogged with multifarious relics and junk. A pickup truck with a hood over its bed, the whole heap painted gunmetal gray except for the patriotic red, white and blue mudflaps. A decaying blue Mercury (a '62 or '63). A Ronald Reagan lawn jockey. A wooden burro painted red and black. An octagonal road sign with a toothless moronic smile-face painted on it. Potted cacti. Bushel baskets and rain barrels and empty jugs and a partially unraveled sheet of wire fencing. Croquet mallets and Wiffle ball bats and rubber snakes dangling from tree limbs like jumbo wind chimes. A rusty aqua-and-cream Chevy, also of early '60s vintage, up on blocks. A small hill of bricks and concrete chunks and plaster rubble. An oasis of beige weeds next to the Chevy. A plastic wading pool with a toy submarine a-slosh in an inch of rainwater and matted leaves. A totally rusted backhoe.

"The yard definitely has texture," I said.

We cast off our lethargy when hunger pangs hit us and dressed up in our Saturday-night finery. I wore my lightweight dove-gray jacket, my impressionist lily-pad tie and my crisp white sailor pants, and the women were resplendent in their summer dresses. We drove to Chagrin Falls and walked 154 around until twilight fell, showing

Marge the sights. The water boomed down its stone chute, the sound mixed with the voices of children playing in the park.

I decided to stymie Jane by drinking milk with my meal, although the meat and potatoes cried out for wine. I poured red wine for Marge and Jane and watched them eat, pleased with myself. Yet the buds in my tongue sobbed for vino.

On the drive back to the lake the forestland hummed with the vibration of massed insect choirs. A billion pulsing bugs. Jane pushed up the seat divider and sat snug against me, allowing Marge to squeeze into the front seat with us. I could smell their skin and hair and perfume. I felt an intense déjà vu of a nocturnal country ride—the bare legs of girls, the feel of the cooling upholstery, the radiant greenery in the sweeping headlights, the tribes of insects abuzz in the darkness, and my erection quickening in my pants. Driving, dreaming, in love.

Lake Piney was devoid of weekend uproar. Buster's pickup truck was gone and his house dark. Jane had her boombox, which we set up in Marge's cabin. We drank iced tea and listened to the Roches' *Keep on Doing* and Van Morrison's *Moondance* and NRBQ's *Tap Dancing Bats*. Despite lacking a date on Saturday night, Marge didn't seem mopey. It unnerved me that some women could so easily cope without romance. I was a miserable wreck without a woman. Marge was a big, calm, self-possessed girl, moving her lips to the sound of Van Morrison, brushing her toes along the floorboards.

We split up at one A.M. Marge put the headphones on to listen to the Bongos' *Drums Along the Hudson*—I was trying to improve her taste incrementally, and she was at least willing to try something new. When Jane and I returned to our cabin, I turned the fan on, slammed a few mosquitoes with Buster's newspaper, and joined Jane for ablutions and teeth-scouring.

I undressed and slipped under the sheet and watched Jane take off her dress and frilly undies. There couldn't be many women on the planet who were as beautiful as Jane. Sober and resolute and electrically aroused, I wooed her far into the night.

SUNDAY HAVOC

$\mathcal{T}$he sound of laughter, guttural and spasmodic, woke me up. Jane moaned softly and bunched the sheet around her shoulders. She had me pinned on the inside against the wall, which was the brown-varnish color of fried chicken. I slipped out of bed at the bottom and pulled on my cutoffs and walked out onto the porch scratching myself.

Buster stood beneath a fake rubber snake talking and gesturing to a portly black dude dressed in a white suit and white beret and white tasseled loafers.

"We got us a interloper, Walker. Slip over here and have a swig of Bloody Mary, kid."

I walked barefoot across the lawn, up on my toes in anticipation of glass shards, and took the jar from Buster. It was heavy on the Tabasco and heavier on the vodka.

"We some heathen rascals, drinkin' this concoction on a Sunday mornin', huh," the black man said.

I choked a little and passed the jar to Buster.

"Bud, this here's Walker Busby. A newspaper tycoon and grand poobah of the Afro-American knuckleheads."

Walker gave me a thick warm mitt to shake and laughed his engine-misfiring, rough hee-haw of a laugh. Buster added his own redneck har-har-har, like a mule with a vibrator up its ass, and I couldn't help smiling.

"Buster gonna get the mau-mau treatment he don't mend his ways. I tole him, he don't listen."

"How's those two sweeties doin', Bud? Purrin' like kittens or scratchin' on your post?"

"Jane's purring. I'm not sure about Marge. Lake Piney isn't exactly the fun-in-Acapulco deal she was hoping for."

"I'll make it up to her. Or dislocate a joint tryin'... Walker, this little pooter's got more white women than he knows what to do with."

I shook my head. "Better renew the subscription to your favorite stroke book, Buster. I got all the real women cornered."

"We'll see. We'll see. Wake 'em up and get 'em over here. I got grub—eggs à la Buster and all the trimmin's."

"I don't know, Buster. We were thinking about the buffet at the inn. A little elegance."

"Elegance my rosy-red asshole! I'll shoot your tires out! You ain't goin' nowhere!"

Jane thumped down the porch steps in her clogs. She wore tight pink shorts and a white cotton jersey.

"Get over here and settle this thing, sweet cakes," Buster hollered. "This pudwhopper boyfriend of yours is liftin' his leg and squirtin' on Buster's hospitality."

Jane thumped over and put her arm around my waist. "Now what?"

"I got omelets, I got hashbrowns, I got muffins, I got coffee—but Bud says no. Piss on that. He wants a silk tablecloth and a plastic flower in a vase and a waiter dressed like Uncle Ben."

"Be startin' with that Uncle Ben business, I'll burn your barn," Walker said. He took off his beret and slapped Buster with it.

"You know I'm on your side when the darky rebellion busts out, Walker. Look at my lips! My ancestors were mingling with yours during the underground railway days. Hell, I'm at least one-eighth coon and it's my best eighth. Let's get whitey together. I got a whole list of white grapenuts I'd like t'lynch."

"You're whiter than a marshmallow and you know it, Buster."

"Don't have a fit, Buster," Jane said. "We'll eat your slop. I don't know about Marge, though. She might need more 157 sleep."

"Sleep's over." Buster grabbed a rusty mallet, scurried over to Marge's cabin, and gonged the door frame. "Up and at 'em, Marge. Wash your kisser, take a tinkle, put some duds on. Breakfast in twenty minutes. Sour-apple crêpes, rutabaga fritters, prize hog bacon, whatever you want..."

Jane sighed. "Sorry, everybody."

"Miss Jane, Mister Bud—it was an enchantment." We shook hands with Walker. He got in his convertible and peeled out.

"One-eighth! Never deny it!" Buster yelled at him.

We spent our twenty-minute stay of execution strolling around the grounds. There were jalopies parked in front of all but one cabin. All the vacationers were late sleepers except for a church-going couple who almost flattened us backing out in their Buick. Past cabin #14 was a field filled with wildflowers and sumac and dragonflies and Monarch butterflies.

When we returned to our cabin, Marge was sitting on our stoop brushing her hair. "Breakfast with Buster, then what? An afternoon at the cockfights?"

"I think they're more into illegal dogfights out here in the boonies, Marge," I said.

Spatula in hand, Buster met us at the door of his house, which had a bunch of lavender and yellow RUTABAGA CONSCIOUSNESS decals pasted on it. He led us through the living room, which was dominated by a 36" screen TV with a polka show playing fuzzily, the sound turned down. Pearl LaRoca was parked in a BarcaLounger with the Sunday funnies held up to her squinting gaze. She had a dish towel tucked in the neckline of her dress and a bowl of gruel, jam and milk on a tray. She dipped a toast crust into the gruel and ignored us.

"Don't distract Ma when she's studyin' *Beetle Bailey*." Buster guided us through the kitchen and onto a screened porch. Stacks of hot-rod and gun-collector and *Analog* magazines took up two-thirds of the floor space. Buster had a card table set for four—paper Howard Johnson's placemats and plastic silverware.

"Take the seat with the special heinie cushion, Marge. I don't want you gettin' a dent." Buster seated her with a flourish. He served outsized blueberry muffins scabbed with melted brown sugar, a green chili, scallion, jalapeño cheese and Red Devil sauce omelet, potatoes fried in Crisco, and strong coffee. My stomach felt like hardening cement after a few bites, but I cleaned my plate along with everybody else.

Buster had some brandy to enliven the coffee. Jane and I refused, but Marge took a hit.

"Pretty decent eats for an unskilled white boy to whip up, doncha think?" A toothpick seesawed in his fat lips.

"Not bad," I said. "How come Walker didn't stay?"

"Ah, Walker's got a scruple or two left. Won't break bread with trash like Buster."

Buster gave us a tour of his den, which was a converted garage. He had hundreds more magazines piled in the grease trap, and there were hoes and shovels against the wall. His bookshelves overflowed with sci-fi paperbacks and a sprinkling of quality fiction—*Huckleberry Finn, The Confidence Man, A Death in the Family.*

"Where's all your Henry James, Buster?" Jane asked.

"Got it hid beneath my lid." He conked his spherical noggin.

There was an ancient Underwood typewriter and manuscripts in boxes and manila folders. Next to the typewriter was a CB unit, which crackled just as I noticed it.

Buster hoisted the receiver. "This is the Rock."

"Rock, this is Juice Boy. I'm over on Falls Road and I got a seventeen and never seen who can't believe her luck. Chewin' a big wad of pink gum and makin' googoo eyes at the Boy. Is cabin number fourteen spruce?"

"All spickied up, Jug Brain. You owe me two eighteens now, do you copy?"

"Right-o, Rock Head. Be by in fifteen with the seventeen."

"No sirens now, Jail Butt. They upset Ma."

"I copy."

159

Buster hung up. "Wish I had time for a reading, kids. I'd bust out my skull and my cape. Got me a thriller started that might give you all a tingle in the tingly place." He shuffled a pile of pages and tossed them back on his desk.

"Here's the setup. Woman meets the man of her dreams. Real suave mammyjammer. She's a librarian-type but she wears black undies, she's got the margarita mix in the cupboard, she's rentin' Richard Gere tapes—that kinda thing…She moves in with her new guy. Immaculate house, shade trees, swimmin' pool with the anti-piss twenty-four-hour circulation doodad attachment. Everything's peachy, but the first time she's alone in the house, she sneaks out in the garage to nose around. There's a tarpaulin over a pile of boxes. She takes it off. Each box is marked in black marker—1995, 1996, 1997, so on. The seven in '97 has got that slanty line through it like maybe this guy's some kind of Swedish fucker even though he don't look Swedish. Buster likes that detail, he does…So she gets a knife and slits open the 1997 carton. There's a *Time* magazine on top. Some jug-eared jamoke she's never heard of on the cover. December 31, 1997 issue. She's gettin' the willies now. She turns around and there's her fella standing in the doorway with a little ferret grin on his face. And he's munchin' a raw pork chop…That's just the first ten pages. It'll go at least four hundred. I got flyin' pyramids, I got space dogs that look like Benji only they'll eat your face, I got a homing device in a microchip in the president's head, I got striptease girls who start killin' the customers 'cause of auto-suggestion…"

"Sounds too much like the standard autobiographical first novel," I said.

"Uhn-huh…Let me ask you a question, mister smart guy. What's your religious and ethnic persuasion?"

"I'm not persuaded by any known religion, Buster. And I'm half Welsh and half Jewish."

"Hmmm. Don't let on to ma about the Jew half or we'll have a pogrom on a pogo stick."

"I'm half Jewish myself," Marge said. "Should we look for a storm cellar to hide in? Is there gonna be a black-shirt rally in the yard this afternoon, Buster?"

"Hell noooo. Ma just had an incident or two that soured her on Hebrews. Got rooked on a chinchilla fur transaction back in 1957 and never got over it."

In the kitchen Buster rummaged through a cabinet until he found a fresh toothpick.

"Stay out of my Fig Newtons!" Pearl yelled.

"They're safe, ma!" Buster winked at us. "Ma don't trust it when she hears a cupboard door open. She maintains eternal vigilance over her cookie supply."

As we cut through the parlor, crystal jiggling and dancing on the sideboard, a cop car pulled into the yard. Buster hotfooted it across the porch and greeted the cop, who had a blond crewcut and mirror shades. There was a girl in a yellow blouse and yellow hip huggers sitting on the front seat. She blew a large bubble and let it collapse back on her lips. Buster gave the cop a key, and he got back in his car and drove past our cabin and down to the end of the lane and parked.

"The laws can be our friends, kids." Buster did a fast, clumsy shuffle in the dirt. "Junior's a pretty friendly guy when you can catch him off duty."

"Thanks for breakfast, Buster," I said. "We're off to see some nature."

"Let me pack you all some bonus muffins."

I held up my hand: Stop. "Not necessary. We're fine."

"Buster's muffinbusters too hearty for your all's delicate tummies? I'm wounded. Next time I'll sock in somea those two-ounce croissants."

"Lighten up, Buster," Jane said.

"Drive careful now. Junior hates a speeder." He veered over to a scrap heap and hefted a chunk of metal.

We loaded up Marge's car and let her drive. At the arboretum we bumped into Walker Busby on the trail. Still spiffy in his Sunday threads, he had binoculars and a *Peterson Field Guide to Eastern Birds.*

I introduced Marge and she got on Walker's good side by saying, "That's a sharp-looking lid, Walker."

Walker removed his beret and examined it. He chuckled. "Either those Bloody Mamas of Buster's got to me or I just seen a Bolivian condor...You like this old hat, huh darlin'? Here." He set the beret on Marge's crown of honey-blonde hair.

Marge took the binoculars and peered up into a tree. "That's a chickenhawk, I think, Walker."

"I'll be damn. He been hawkin' some Kentucky Fried he so big."

"Do you print Buster's newspaper, Walker?" Jane asked.

"I'm not *pure* fool, darlin'. That's a money-loser, that thing. I shunt some advertisin' Buster's way, that's all. I worked with Buster's daddy out on Kinsman there. Back in fiffy-five, fiffy-six. I liked that white man. Donated blood to me when I got hurt. Man slashed me upside the hip with a fish slicer. Nasty little peckerwood. All kinds of white folks, I met 'em all. Some'll cut a man, some'll shake his hand."

Walker followed the flight of the chickenhawk, soaring and dipping into another grove of trees.

"You good people aren't gettin' involved with Buster, are you? Just rentin' a cabin?"

"That's all," Jane said.

"If he starts mentionin' invest in this, invest in that—you say no. Him 'n' Junior Budlong's well on the way to Chapter Eleven. Opened them a Chinese restaurant in a strip mall out on the edge of Amishville last month. Hired a buncha big old Polish waitresses with the B-52 hairdos. Man can't even get a cuppa green tea in there. Buster got a deal on RC Cola. Truck tipped over, and every can's got the fizzies. Some shitheel at the wholesaler's cut him a deal on this explodin' RC. Only drink on the menu besides water...That's their latest get-rich business. Drivin' range ain't worth shee-it. Condos got termites in there eatin' like a free-for-all. Junior would take a five-dollar bribe from John Dillinger, he's so desperate."

162

"Thanks for the advice," I said. "I don't think Buster sees us as investors, though."

"We're more like whipping boys," Marge said.

"Whipping persons," Jane said. She liked to twit me with unisex feminist jargon.

Walker let a deeper hee-haw. "He's all mouf an' no whip. You best stay clear of his mama, though—oooo-weee, she's hateful. Bad old buzzard of a white lady."

"We hear ya."

We tagged along with Walker for another hour, then drove over to the reservoir for a swim. The changing room smelled like a musty jockstrap, and every preadolescent brat in creation was traipsing around the beach, but the water felt wonderful. Some yahoos did cannonballs off the wooden float. They tugged their trunks low and bobbed their bare asses above the water. "Red eye!" they yelled, as one skinny-assed kid dolphined up and spread his cheeks. "Quit that red eye," a lifeguard chastised through a bullhorn.

"Looks like your kind of crowd, Bud. Whyncha go play with 'em."

"I might."

We drove back to Lake Piney at five o'clock. Two minutes after we arrived Zak's car pulled in, trailed by Junior Budlong. Buster stood in his yard, arms folded and grinning.

Junior walked the slow, menacing, theatrical walk of a cliché movie cop. He crept over into our yard and said to me, "You acquainted with these two knotheads, Mr. Carew?"

"Yeah."

"I apprehended Mr. Tony here drinking from an open beer container in a moving vehicle, and he ain't got enough green to pay his fine."

Buster toddled over to eavesdrop and ogle the girls in their damp bikinis. Junior's head swiveled, also, in a bikini-scan.

"Wasn't Zak driving, though?"

"Makes no difference. County ordinance against partaking in a moving vehicle. It applies to passengers. Skateboarder latches on to your bumper with a brew in his hand, we'll fine you. I believe Mr. Zak just killed a can and rolled it under the seat as I come up on 'em, but I'll let that slide. The fine's forty on the spot or eighty later. Plus we ask a donation for the local Animal Protective League, which is in the shitter financially."

"We got feral cats all over hell," Buster said. "That's why Junior asks for citizen help. We catch 'em, clean 'em up, declaw 'em, nut 'em and pass 'em on to the deprived kids of the county. Some little drooler gets a kitty, he lights up like a drunk's nose."

"You need forty plus what, then?" I said, sweat beginning to trickle down my armpits. A uniform could make me sweat quicker than a sauna could.

"*Eighty* plus *fifty,* we'll call it. When an offender can't scrape together the forty at the scene of the initial offense, he goes automatically to the 'later' status."

"A hundred thirty bucks for a beer, huh?" Jane pirouetted with her towel wrapped around her, grimacing at Marge. Junior moved his big predatory head to watch her.

"I got seven and Zak's got four," Tony said, gouging his heel into the loose dirt of the chicken-scratch yard. "We only need one-nineteen."

"Spic and Span on the math," Buster said. "These boys aren't too screw-loose, Junior. You won't have to breathalize 'em."

"Shut up. I'll breathalize your mama."

Buster's lips bulged in a pout. He said nothing.

I took out my wallet and gave Tony six twenties.

"Thanks Bud." He grubbed together ten wrinkled singles and gave the bills in a wad to Junior.

"Be thankful I don't write you fuzzballs up."

"We thankful, massuh," Zak said.

Junior shifted his neck in his collar. "Boy, I see your nose has been busted in the past. I'll bust it again."

"He apologizes, Officer Budlong," I said. "I'll see they both behave from here on out."

"I'll hold you to it. I ever catch these squirts swilling beer on a county road again, it'll be two hundred and sixty smackers plus ten days in the county bugpit. That's an experience they don't wanna have, believe me."

Junior strolled back slow-mo to his cruiser, threw it into reverse with the cherry-top blinking and sped away.

"Junior's a steam kettle today," Buster said. "Musta got outta bed with his ass hairs crooked."

"Does he keep a cigar box on the front seat for the 'fines'?" Jane said. "You jerks are probably lucky that you're not a little cuter. He might've taken you down to cabin fourteen for a party."

"What a fuckwad," Tony said. "He pulled out of a concealed turnoff and whizzed past us to see us drinkin' at all. We weren't speeding or weaving or anything."

"I hope you can borrow one-twenty from your old man, Tony. I hate to be a shit, but I'm gonna need that money."

"I'll get it. Thanks for helping out."

Buster fetched a six-pack of Budweiser and gave everybody a beer. Breakfast had satisfied our nutritional requirement for the day, so we decided to skip dinner and take in a local band at a roadhouse out on 303.

Buster declared the band "too snot-nose New Wave for me" and declined to join us. To mollify Zak and Tony, who continued to bitch about their bad fortune, I rode in their car. Jane and Marge followed us in the Toyota. The parking lot was packed and we had to park in a field next door. Beneath a sign that said CLEM'S LOUNGE, a humanoid cowboy dripped green neon droplets from his grizzled neon face, as he drew his gun out and reholstered it endlessly in a back and forth white-hot neon twitch.

We took a booth as far away from the stage as we could get and ordered two pitchers of draft beer. The waitress had a beehive and might have been moonlighting from Buster and Junior's Amish chop-suey joint.

Three Squirt Dog, the band, set up its equipment. The fiddle player sawed a few licks. They were dressed like migrant cabbage pickers—loose, double-cuffed jeans, blue work shirts, and black polio shoes. In a buzz of feedback they started playing. Most of their lyrics were incomprehensible, and the bass was jacked up in the sound mix like a giant's heartbeat, but they weren't bad.

Five songs into the set, the singer-guitarist announced, "This one's dedicated to all you dumbshits spending your paycheck on beer and pretzels and Clem's roadkill burritos—'I Never Bring Home the Bacon, but I Always Bring Home the Meat.' "

They kept getting squirrelier. They sang "My Heroes Have Always Been Transvestites" and "Found Her F-Spot, Found Her H-Spot, Still Ain't Found Her G-Spot." They covered Alice Cooper's "No More Mr. Nice Guy" and Hank Williams's "Kawliga." We kept ordering more pitchers, getting into the prankish spirit of the band. To my surprise no one in the bar jeered or threw a bottle or demanded a Lynyrd Skynyrd medley. They even called out the titles of old Three Squirt tunes, egging them on.

"Must be the house band," I said between songs. "We could be in on history."

The front man deferred to the fiddle player on one song, and he gave its title as "I Dreamed I Was Sleeping with Rosanna Arquette and Then I Woke Up and I Wasn't" or something like that.

Between sets they had their own acoustic tribute band, Enraged Pink Clams, who did alternate versions of four previous Three Squirt songs and a cover of their "Kawliga" cover. The singer wore a wet apron—I think he was the house dishwasher.

We lingered for the second set and left at ten o'clock, our heads swarming like amplifiers on the fritz. I got in   Marge's car and snuggled up next to

Jane. Tony and Zak followed us. A truck whipped around us and Marge cut the wheel to let it pass, gravel spitting over the berm. Jane craned her neck and groaned. "Tony went into the ditch."

Marge braked and made a U-turn and pulled over next to the accident. Tony had probably insisted on driving because he was marginally less drunk than Zak. The car was tilted half in and half out of a deep ditch.

We got out and watched Zak slide like an otter through the pass-enger side window. Tony emerged behind him, cursing as he hit the weeds.

"Are you dribbleshits okay?" I could feel the money melting in my wallet.

"Yeah. The fuckers brushed me on the door and blew me right off the road. I couldn't hear what they were yelling."

"Cool down. We'll have to get a tow truck t'get you outta there."

"Christ! I'm gonna end up in debtor's prison. You have to split this one with me, Zak. Your power steering's fucked."

"Aaahhh." Zak staggered, his head drooping.

"Look what's coming," Marge said.

Up the dark highway rode a police car, red light whirling. It stopped in the gravel and out climbed Junior Budlong.

"Fuck! He's bionic," Tony said. "I can't handle this."

"Shut up and let me do the talking. He already despises you guys. I think he just dislikes me."

Junior stood with his hands on his hips. He had switched from black to orange wraparound shades. His uniform was still perfectly pressed, his tie centered.

"Some people never learn their ABC's." He let his arms dangle, as if he might pull his pistol and fire.

"Junior, a truck ran them off the road. It almost sideswiped our car too."

"Sure, sure. There's always a phantom truck. Probably had a headless ghost driving it. What we got here is not trucks—it's beer. I can smell beer fumes ten yards away. I oughta run you all in and get an award from the chief and the M.A.D.D. mothers. You people are hopeless."

"Let me straighten this out. We had a few beers. Hell, we're tourists. We're helping the local economy. We're not drunk. It'd be a good PR move on your part to just call us a tow truck."

"Don't gall me, boy. Where'd you get the idea I'm in the PR business?"

I rubbed my sweaty forehead and mashed a sweat-sponging bug. "All right then. How much will it cost us?"

"How much you got?"

My blood heated. I still had about $300, but I *needed* it to spend on happier revels. "About a hundred," I said softly.

"We've got some money," Jane said sharply.

"Keep quiet, Miss Pink Pants. We'll settle this."

I thought how enjoyable it would be to massage Junior's prostate with his nightstick, but I said calmly, "Take the hundred, Junior. Get some cats spayed. Buy some balloons for the county orphans. I'd appreciate it. Buster'd appreciate it."

"Buster's an affliction. Mention his name again and I'll run you down to the county lockup and have 'em shave your head."

I could hear Zak puking in the weeds.

Marge broke the lull. "My dad's a lawyer. I could call him. These shakedown tactics are outrageous even for a crooked hick cop."

Junior scanned his orange shades toward Marge. "Now Bubblebutt here gets mouthy with me. The fine just went up to two hundred. Better pool your funds or I'll call the wagon."

"Marge is right," Jane said. "Let's go make that call." She kicked gravel and glared at Junior. A truck whooshed past us, several rubberneckers dangling off the bed.

"What's the use." I took out my wallet, counted ten twenties, and gave them to Junior.

"What's this shit? I thought you were down to your last hundred."

I shrugged.

"Show me your wallet."

I mustered every ounce of self-control, then slipped out my wallet and handed it to Junior. He counted the remaining bills.

"You had two-ninety-four, liar."

"What's the fine for lying?"

"Fifty." He peeled off two twenties and a ten. He reached the wallet behind me and jammed it into my hip pocket and walloped me on the flank.

"Okay, candyass. The tow truck shouldn't run you more than forty bucks. You'll have enough left over to get a couple Egg McMuffins tomorrow morning."

He strolled slowly to his car, revved the engine, cruised very slowly a hundred yards, and stopped. A red mist blew from his tailpipe. He waited a minute and then kept going.

"I'll drive to a gas station and get a tow truck to come," Marge said. "Sorry I cost you the extra hundred, Bud."

"He would've got it, anyway. You were brave to speak up. You too, baby." I embraced Jane, and she was writhing with fury. After Marge left, Tony and Zak avoided us, squatting in the weeds by the rear bumper of Zak's car and muttering darkly.

"I've heard about people who crawled out from under rocks," Jane said. "But this guy must've been *evicted* by the other slime that lives under the rock."

CORNCOBBING

JUNIOR

*W*e waited until after Labor Day to hatch a counterplot. I drove Jane to Pittsburgh and helped her move into her senior-year quarters, a garish two-bedroom apartment with a pink shag rug the texture of a hooker's coat and a Willie Stargell poster above the fridge. Dale, her roommate, was a pale-blonde, almost albino, little Chiclet—a 97-pound Florida girl whose stepmother shelved books at the college library. Dale played that goddamn *Synchronicity* album over and over as Jane and I loved ourselves dizzy in her room. I developed a Pavlovian twitch whenever I heard the xylophonelike sound at the beginning of "King of Pain."

Back home, we staked out Junior's private gouging preserve in shifts. Zak followed Junior home from the station one night. Perfect setup for us: the slug lived on a backstreet, his cottage set two hundred yards into the bug-clouded woods. I buttonholed Billy and O.T., who happily signed on as the fourth and fifth muskeeters. From a handy construction dump the Burdette boys supplied the dirt.

We knew that Junior was working three-to-midnight shifts. We backed up his narrow driveway at six o'clock, Billy yeehawing as he peeled gravel like grapeshot into the weeds. Zak and Tony backed their revengemobile in behind us. We piled Junior's mondo-ugly furniture into his empty two-car garage. By dusk we packed a three-inch layer of dirt on every square foot of floor space in his denuded pad.

Zak found a boxful of *Juggs* and *40 Plus* and *Bra Busters* mags in Junior's closet. We slathered the living room wall with glue and slapped them up page by page. We marveled at the biker mama with the Ghidra and Rodan tattoos.

Tony found $600 in tens and twenties in a wooden jewelry box. It would bankroll our post-vandalism party and repay the $280 Tony still owed me. On a hunch I probed an empty Kleenex box on the bedroom floor and plucked out a packet of snapshots—candid pics of waylaid teenage girls.

What a big foul corn-encrusted shit-torpedo this guy was.

We all wore surgical gloves and cheap disposable bathing clogs. No prints, no fiber evidence. Billy and O.T. knocked out all the screens. In the mosquito-laden twilight we hooked up the hose and went from window to window and hosed that puppy down. Junior's five-room dance floor went from mud slab to paste to oozing bog.

At 10:00 I screwed the sprinkler attachment on the nozzle and snaked it into the living room and turned it on HIGH. Hip-hopping around the packed garage like a naked troll, Billy shook skunk musk on Junior's furniture collection. We hosed off his musk-spattered feet, he squeezed his flab back into his duds and we hightailed out of there.

"Too bad we don't have some hot stones, so we could get the bubblin' volcanic mud effect," Billy said.

On the way home we found a drive-through beverage store and stopped to buy two cases of wide-mouthed Mickey's. We convoyed home and gathered in the Burdettes' backyard and guzzled beer and congratulated ourselves on the righteousness and efficiency of our outing.

"Satisfied now?" O.T. asked.

"Not quite," I said. "I'd still like to see the bastard squirming up close and personal. What we did tonight'll just inconvenience him."

"You got a funny way of definin' 'inconvenience.' How'd you like t'come home dog-ass tired and find a swamp where your house used t'be?"

"I'm not complaining. You men did yeoman work. It just lacks that final iota of satisfaction. Conceptually."

"I got a brain bubble," Zak said, fingering the rim of his beer bottle. "I'll talk to Pickle Juice at work tomorrow and get back to you."

The next day I scrawled a letter *171* to Junior, slanting my alphabet left

and right, making it big and small, using pens and crayons—DEAR JUNIOR—
HOPE U ENJOYED YR MUDHUMP. U LEAVE YR FILTHY COP PAWS OFF
OUR DAWTER LUGENE OR WE GON SKIN & SALT YR BUTT—BUFORD.
P.S. WE MITE FIREBOMB YR ROOTABAGA FARM FROM OUR
CROPDUSTER. U BEST LAY IN SOME ANTI AIRCRAFT GUNZ.

I drove out to the rural postal station next to the bait shop on 303 to mail the
letter. Let Junior worry about local enemies. I'm sure he had a bunch.

Thursday night Zak and Tony and I paid a visit to Pickle Juice. He lived in a brick
apartment building near the old Masonic Temple on Euclid Avenue. In the ratty
courtyard two tenants were breeding their poodles. The dogs, both leashed, were tied
and panting, butt to butt, as a peanut gallery of young Hispanics watched from the
stoop.

"Hey bro', lay a beer on me," said a guy in a strap T-shirt and porkpie hat as we
tried to squeeze into the building. I gave him a Rolling Rock.

Pickle Juice lived on the third floor. He had a Mr. T poster taped to his door. He
let us in, stroking his handlebar mustache, loose suspenders hanging to his thighs.
Dirty laundry was scattered everywhere, and a George Clinton record played on the
stereo.

"Picky Juice," Zak said. "Have a beer."

Zak explained the nature of our mission. Pickle Juice licked foam from his
mustache. "Commando style might be the best way to go. My cousin drives a UPS
truck—I'll dummy up a package and go out there with him to the mudhole and see
what the setup is."

Two days later we met in Dewey's breezeway. "Well, he's got a big black dog on
a chain that barks like a motherfucker. He's got zero furniture, just a mattress to sleep
on. Floors look clean. Hell, they're cleaner than the floors in my apartment. Wallpaper
in the living room looks a little splotchy where he tore down the tit pictures."

"No security system?" Tony said.

"What's left to secure?"

"You leave the package?"

"Oh yeah."

"What was in it?"

"Deck of gay pornographic playing cards my cousin happened to have handy."

"If you're really up for this," I said, "let's go see him on Saturday night."

Pickle Juice smiled. "Could be fun."

It rained all day Saturday. We met at Pickle Juice's and climbed into his van. We donned black jumpsuits, Oakland Raider caps, and black boots. We bootblacked our faces, slapped hands and split for the country.

Pickle Juice had been a Black Knight Commando since '77, though the gang had mostly gone underground in the '80s. Their agenda of mischief included egging and depantsing politicians in parking lots, chopping down neon signs with insulated buzzsaws, painting graffiti on business establishments that had swindled them or refused them service. They always dressed in their knucklehead occidental ninja garb.

Through the wet countryside we rode, singing a cappella punk medleys. We backed up Junior's driveway at 11:30. We were fairly beered up but alert. We opened the garage, which reeked of skunk juice *and* disinfectant. We backed in and parked and shut the door behind us. No sign of the black mutt.

It was a long wait, drinking two warm beers apiece, until Junior arrived at 1:30. He parked in a puddle and scampered inside. I listened at the door that led into the kitchen. When the shower came on, I signaled and we went Indian file through the jimmied door into the kitchen and across the bare living room and up the hall past the bathroom.

Junior had a single goose-necked lamp in his bedroom. His uniform and six-shooter and holster were draped over a chair. I groped in his pants and found his wallet and pocketed it in my jumpsuit.

173

The shower stopped. When Junior slogged into the bedroom, toweling himself dry, Pickle Juice lassoed him.

"Fucky ducky, we caught a white man."

As Junior bellowed and twisted, Tony bagged his head and sashed it. As Junior squirmed, Pickle Juice spritzed him in his pidgin-Oriental voice.

"Most applopliate we bag white virrain with his tiny biddy exposed. Please to plostlate him." Tony, Zak and I pitched the heavy bastard onto the mattress and pinned him. "Is a high clime to be clamming such a woffless biddy into so many innocent girrs of the alea. Is that not so, Wang?"

"Ah so."

"Two possibirities for punishments. One—we rop off the offending biddy and take it to county office for fifty-cent biddy bounty. Two—we subject offending white boy to dousing celemony. We shall vote on it. Wang?"

"One."

"Fang?"

"Two."

"Hang?"

"Two."

"I prefuh two also. Lemove bag from ugry mug, Wang, as I get my baroons."

Zak put his boot on Junior's ear when, debagged, he started to squawk.

"Shut up, white dog, or we do numbuh one slashermetrics."

Pickle Juice returned with three balloons in a shopping bag. He poised one over Junior's head. "Do not peek, flour-face. Could become brind man." He poked the fabric with a hatpin, releasing pickle brine and old jism into Junior's hair.

He dangled and poked the second balloon: liquefied poodle shit.

"Numbuh thlee baroon the best." Pickle Juice punctured it, and we all gagged: mink musk. "Wang, Fang, Hang. Tie the stinky infidel so we can be leaving in peace."

We used cord to hogtie Junior.

174

"Now we say so longa, Mistuh June-yuh. Advice to you—ceribacy, honor, obedience. No more ficky ficky. If so, we come back and slice off biddy in numbuh-one method."

We removed the tires from Junior's car, rolled them into the wet weeds, and mink-musked his upholstery. We sailed up the dripping lane and headed home.

"Slow down," I warned Pickle Juice, who chugged along on his Black Knight Commando adrenaline rush. "Be a bitch if some gung-ho cop pulled us over. We'd have to go through this whole process again."

WEEKEND
BLISS

*T*he following Friday I left Dewey's store and ramrodded to Pittsburgh and checked into a downtown hotel. I put a dozen yellow roses in a vase on the bed table and socked a bottle of juice in the ice bucket. I took the hilly streets to Jane's apartment and found her and Dale and Dale's boyfriend Rudy watching the last segment of *Ride the High Country* on TV. It was one of my favorite movies and I regretted missing the mining-camp scenes and the gun battles. I sat respectfully, my heart quaking as I touched Jane for the first time in twelve days, and watched Joel McCrea die.

Jane packed a small bag, said, "See you guys Monday," and we left. As ugly as they all are, all cities nevertheless glitter at night. Pittsburgh had its river lights and lambent barges, its ruby lanterns and emerald coronas, its electric fireflies. From our window on the sixteenth floor we beheld the tiers of soft yellow lights in the hills and brilliant traffic slipstreams leaving the city. I kissed Jane on the neck and held her around the waist, inhaling the smell of her hair and perfume and bewitching female secretions.

We took a long bath in the big tub. Jane played the water taps with her nimble slender toes like a typist. I washed every plane and cranny of her scrumptious body. She turned to sit on my submerged lap and I kissed her bullet-hard nipples. Jane was flushed and pink from the hot water and our closeness. Her provocative eyes challenged me to do something, so I showed her my version of the Loch Ness monster.

"This rascal's ready to get out on land and do some rampagin'." We slopped so much water on the floor that we had to use every towel in the joint to sop it up.

It was after midnight when we got in bed. Neither of us was really tired. We were keyed up by the luxury and privacy. We lay enfolded in the partial dark, light playing from the sky on the closed beige drapes.

"How's Marge?"

"Still pissed off. She's a paralegal for her daddy, starting this week. She wants to sic the law on Junior."

"Junior *is* the law. Besides, it won't be necessary. Vengeance is ours, saith the drunken drivers." I told Jane about how we'd redesigned Junior's digs and christened him in the Three Unholy Fluids Ceremony.

"Hell, he's a generous guy. He's even paying for our room this weekend."

"You guys might end up on a chain gang."

"Never happen. Officially, we spent those two evenings watching *It's Alive* and *It's Alive 2* with Rayford and Bonnie, and playing a round-robin Scrabble tournament that lasted all night Saturday. We got sworn testimony if we ever need it. Junior's enemies are legion. It'll take the FBI a year just t'screen 'em all."

"*Skunk* musk, though?" Jane chortled a deep rough chortle. "That's fairly harsh."

"Hey, the mink musk was just as putrid, believe it or not. We're prepared to break out the ultimate stink next time. We'll take a sack of Sam's shit out there and hit him with it."

"Junior may become an even worse rogue now."

"I doubt it. We gave him pause, I'm sure. You shoulda seen that furniture. It was an aesthetic necessity to destroy it. Zebra-pattern couch, fart-faced cherubs on the chiffonier, pea soup–colored chairs...I just hope his home owner's insurance had lapsed."

"Looks like you burned your bridges at Lake Piney."

"Hell no. Let's go back every summer."

Jane tweaked my nipples. "What's up next? You bozos gonna take a custard-pie squad after Reagan?"

"Nah. I feel purged. I'm entering a non-violent phase."

"How 'bout here and now. What are you gonna do for me?"

"I'm gonna make you so cross-eyed happy you'll have to redefine the word *oh-gasm*."

"What a braggart. Show me."

"You know I lubs a challenge." I was caressing Jane's breasts and belly, so taut yet so silken, and her skin was humming like the plateau along a railroad line, just as the 12:20 was hurtling down the tracks toward it.

It was after two A.M. when I got up to get us a drink. We were certainly parched.

"What the hell?" Jane swallowed. "Papaya juice...There's no alcohol in this?"

"Huhn-uh. I'm sober as a Baptist. Except for patriotic holidays maybe. Or weddings and funerals, birthdays of close friends, eclipses and comets...I'm gonna be an artfully scattered drunk."

"What brought on this attack of sobriety? Dewey take you to a Billy Graham crusade?"

"Nope. I just decided to tidy up my act, see how it works...As a lark."

"Are you gonna go completely nuts? Get a real job?"

"Listen up...Dewey's gonna sell the house and move into an apartment with Omar. This real estate development company offered him really good money on his property. They're building estates in the woods behind us, and they can use our house for a command post, and run a road back to the building site...Dewey's gonna take that money and open a second shop out in Lake County. And I'll run that fucker...I'm looking at apartments and small houses in Fairport and Grand River. Nice sleepy little lake towns..."

"A sober little junior businessman. Gonna join the Kiwanis?"

I held Jane's butt cheeks in my hands. "Semi-sober. I got my sweet Jane to intoxicate me." I kissed her, tasting her heat and papaya-flavored saliva. What was this tropical princess, so tan and warm and lithe, doing in Pittsburgh?

"I don't know if I fit the role of standby, part-time intoxicant. My education'll go to waste. I might just abscond with a doctor or a lawyer, I got scads of rich suitors."

"You'd have to move to a different solar system to find anybody who'll love you more than I will, Miz Jane."

She squeezed my hand, lowered it to her thigh. "Yeah. That's the trouble."

"There's no trouble in here. All the trouble in the world is out there beyond our door. In here we're together. Trouble can't find us."

"Men are such doofuses."

"Me?"

"Sometimes. Men as a breed. They need so much coaching. They're remedial."

"Coach away then. Don't you think we'll take instruction?"

"It wouldn't work. You'd backslide. Or you'll pull your hurt-little-boy routine if we say anything even mildly abrasive. Oooo, that wicked ball-busting woman, she won't let me do anything."

"How'd I land in the jerk-pool all the sudden? Tell me what I did?"

"I'm not talking about anything you did. Calm down, little boy. I'm talking about prevalent male attitudes. A woman can teach some jerk how to do the right thing, but he's *still* a jerk. Essen-   tially. *Inside.* He's just learned how to simulate the right moves. It's better to just let him stay a jerk. Then he's transparent and he can't deceive us."

"*Us,* huh? Hoard your feminine wisdom from us jerks. Sounds like a conspiracy theory. Do you really feel this sisterhood solidarity or is it just a tactic?"

"A *tactic?*"

"Ouch!" Jane pinched the bottom fold of my scrotum.

"I really feel it, jerkweed."

"Don't pinch my grapes. And don't misunderstand me, baby. I'm glad you feel it. I love you for it. I'm the luckiest jerk in the world, sore nuts and all."

"It's an insoluble problem, Bud. I don't want to break your spirit, I don't want to domesticate you. I hate those yes-honey, no-honey men. But I don't want you to slip into that mentality that Zak and Tony have, if you can call it a mentality. Zonked stupidity as a life-style..."

"Whew! Now we're getting somewhere. Now I see where the jerk thesis started—Zak and Tony. Okay. On the face of it, they're jerks. But baby, they're not that awful. They're good-hearted people. I've never seen either one of 'em do anything really malicious. I've told you before, they're totally in awe of you. You scare them, and they bumble around acting stupid. It's classic male behavior, I admit it. If either one of 'em got lucky and found a girl with some patience and tolerance, they'd be okay."

"Would you wish Zak on any woman? Or Tony? Mister blitzkrieg fingers. I've heard stories about him." Jane snorted in exasperation.

"Yeah, Tony's been blackballed due to excessively active hands. They both need work. They're fixer-uppers. But don't ask me to badmouth my friends. When I quit playing baseball and got booted out of the fucking jockacracy for good, Zak and Tony were my best friends. I've known Zak since I was eight years old, and he's never badmouthed me once."

"He said you came in your pants when you took Donna Vermiel to see *Urban Cowboy.*"

179

"I *did* come in my pants that night. That was just accurate reporting."

Jane squirmed on the sheet, giggling. "You're just a sperm accident waiting to happen, aren't you?"

"No pinching. And don't ask me to denounce my friends. You can maintain your sisterhood network, and I won't bitch."

"I'm not asking for a denunciation. Just a reappraisal."

"Good. I'll reappraise the dumb fuckers and publish my findings...Let's just love each other as best we can, Jane. I can't do anything more than that. Let's have our weekends, and when you graduate in June we'll go from there."

"Okay."

"Let's not be melancholy."

Jane's hands fondled my ass. "Who's melancholy?"

Without thinking I said, "I wish your parents didn't hate me so virulently."

"They don't! Remove your head from your ass, Bud. One time, one time my dad said something harmless about liking some shitty old record better than today's rock—and you've snubbed him ever since. It's so fucking childish! My parents are pretty liberal, they just don't own a hip record store like Dewey and act like the toastmaster general seven days a week. Mom knows I'm on the pill. She got the bill from Student Health, for God's sake. She never criticized me. She's happy that I'm a good student and that I'm not on drugs like half of the college population. She's hurt that *you* never say two words to her. It's not like my parents are these stuck-up old fuds who're pressuring me not to see you. They'd fucking *embrace* you if you'd give an inch...So Daddy plays his oldies, so what? Didn't Dewey sum up early rock 'n' roll? Shimmy shimmy koko bop, neenie nana nana nunu, a-wop-boppa-lu-bop-a-lim-bam-boom...It's all like spit noises that little kids make in their mouth when they're just googling around...If you grew up in the fifties, you'd probably love the same shit. It's not a moral failing in Daddy because he doesn't sit around in a trance trying to figure out the lyrics to R.E.M. songs...You've got to come down off your snotty, college radio high horse, Bud. My parents are just human."

I was smiling in the dark. I never loved Jane more than when she was pitching a passionate shit-fit. I kissed her on the lips, then held the glass of juice for her to sip.

"Okay, you've trounced me. I'll put in a special memorial Little Anthony and the Imperials section at the new store and invite your dad out for the opening. I'll even grant your hawk-faced mom provisional humanity."

"Don't give me any 'provisional' shit."

"Shhh. You're right. I know you're right. Just don't ask me to get to know Freddie better."

Jane laughed into the pillow. "Freddie's been maligned, too. He just acts monstrous."

"Yeah, all ax murderers just *act* like ax murderers."

"He loves animals. That's his saving grace. He wants to be a vet."

I chuckled. "A vet on the Island of Lost Souls maybe...All this hypothetical fellowship is starting to knock us both woozy."

Jane touched my pecker, which stretched and then sprang up completely. Boinnggg.

"Magic fingers. I'll put a spell on you." Her voice was gruff enough to imitate Screamin' Jay Hawkins.

I pushed the sheet aside and let Jane get atop me and I was instantly inside her, tired and a little sore yet exultant as she romped above me, her hands pressing my chest.

After I came, I drifted asleep, and Jane woke me by hefting my dick again. "Wait a second here. That's a piss hard-on, baby. Let me go drain this devil, and we'll see what's left of him afterwards."

I peed a torrent and then washed my rod under the tap. I was still hard when I got back in bed.

"Okay, Wonder Woman. One more time and then we sleep."

"Knock yourself out, sperm boy."

We made love sideways like underwater dancers, and the final tripwire in my nerve endings thrummed and I flooded Jane convulsively until my legs throbbed and an extra pulse began to beat in my shoulder and I shuddered to a stop.

"Oh my God. This must be criminal, it feels so great. We'll have to go on the lam to escape the fuck-police."

"Uhhhmmmm. Put some gas in the car and let's hit the road."

"First we sleep."

We slept until 11:30, when a maid in a blonde beehive and a salmon-pink uniform unlocked the door and peered over the taut door chain.

"Sorry. Youse guys sleep some more. I'll put the sign up." She shut the door softly. Jane pressed against me, murmuring, and I cradled her in my arms. We drifted asleep again, and in my dream I lay exactly where I was outside the dream: asleep in Jane's arms, warm and safe and sated, like a fortunate boy in his perfect dream of happiness.